The 20th Parallel

I dedicate this book to you, the reader. It is solely for you to interpret.

1. TRIALS

It was dark in my cell but regardless I didn't want to seem awake. I had been in this cell for the latter half of five years as I awaited my final fate. My name is Reggie and yes, this is my life. I was falsely accused of the murder of my wife. For the most part all I could do was just spend my time laying there, thinking about the things that I have done. Along with thinking of how I could have made it out of this place.

The courtroom was quiet, however, it was definitely tense. I remember specifically the judge having a special anguish for this certain case. All I could do was just sit there wearing my bright orange jumpsuit and think about what may happen in the next coming hours. I knew that whatever it may have been would change the rest of my life. The judge looked down with no empathy towards me and my lawyer, I knew exactly what he was thinking. He didn't know what kind of human on this Earth could have committed such a terrible Act. Although, I could only assume that what I thought was going to happen to me was well deserved. I originally lived in Boulder, Colorado.

Life was slow but very easy there as I had not many worries. I went through elementary school, middle school, high school, I even tried getting into some decent College. Everything was nice there. I grew up, learned, and somehow, landed myself in this small concrete room. One night I was out drinking with my friends, which slowly became a normal routine for me. Everything played out as usual until I came across this lady. At an instant, I was especially fond of her. I didn't know exactly how to approach her as I was fairly new to any situation of that type, yeah I wasn't really the best at handling relationships.

Long story short, went up to her and I asked her what she was majoring in. She answered; "Vodka and poetry. Sit down, buy you a sandwich." I thought that she was kidding, due to the fact that I was too out of it and drunk to understand what was going on. So I just accepted it.

"My name is Jessie by the way," she said with mild frustration.

"Nice to meet you, my name's Reggie, but my friends call me Reg," I replied.

"Sure thing Reggie," she said with a smirk.

A few months went by of the same thing happening over and over again.

I guess we just put up with each other. Multiple dates went by and I could only hope that we both enjoyed it. We both drove each other crazy. It was great. One cold night in the summer of 1976, about two months after our two-year anniversary, I asked for her hand in marriage. To my astonishment, She said yes. That was probably the greatest night of my life.

"How do you feel about kids," she asked one chilly day overlooking our Boulder apartment building balcony.

"I don't know, they're small hyper they don't know much and kind of annoying," I answered.

Meanwhile Jessie was trying to get a job somewhere in Denver, however, it was looking Bleak in terms of finding one. Another summer went by and we were etching towards 1977. The plans to have kids have been waylaid by still trying to find a suitable job. I didn't even know where to turn during that time. However, I did start noticing some small problems. I began to notice the small things that bothered Jessie. These were things that I wouldn't think would necessarily bother on a normal person. She would always be anxious over random situations, talking to herself, stressing up a storm about things as small as losing a key.

Even during the rough night, she would stay up until 3 in the morning just thinking of God knows what. I was starting to become worried about her. Worried for us. This same feeling only escalated more over time. One day Jessie went up to me and told me that she thought she had found a suitable job after so long. It was all the way up in New York. Some sort of fashion elementary, a sign of some sort. Always something that she had a keen eye for. I was very skeptical. She told me everything about it. I think, it was one of the first times that I ever saw her feel truly passionate about something.

That alone weighed on me. One side of me wanted her to be happy, but another wanted *us* to be happy. I told her that I didn't know if it would be the right thing to do. It would take some time to figure things out. I guess the time in 1978, I believe it was sometime in October, was an even more somber period for the both of us. Jessie started having a relapse in her problems. This time it was severe. At this point, we decided to go into therapy to get things straightened out. It was a long cold winter that year. And our future plans to potentially have children we're still at the back of our minds.

I decided to let Jessie take the job. It was a long way over to the Big Apple. But I knew that if it would make her happy, then that is what we needed to do. She promised that she would visit promptly, I wasn't even sure if I was ready to accept these terms myself, however. I knew it was for the best. June 28th, 1979, I was out on our back patio just enjoying the Sunshine When I got a call. I had usually personalized each ringtone to determine who was calling me. I had not recognized this one. I grabbed my phone anxiously just to read the caller ID. "Plainsboro Medical Center". It read. I picked it up hesitantly. "Hello?" I was quick to ask.

"Hello, is this Reggie Green?" the man on the other end responded.

"Yes, what is this about," I asked.

"We're just calling you to inform you that your wife Jessie Green has been admitted to us in urgent care. We're so sorry, Sir," he said.

I actually could not even believe what I was hearing. Some part of me almost started to believe it was some type of joke. Some type of disturbing messed up joke. But I knew it was not. I was too outdone to even respond properly.

"How is she? Is she okay? What happened?" I just could not get it all out at once.

"She's unfortunately in critical condition, she's probably going to be here for a while. And unfortunately, we are still trying to find out what exactly happened."

At this point I was getting furious, how could they not know what happened. They just got a patient admitted into the emergency room, and they don't even have any knowledge whatsoever of what happened.

"No disrespect, but this whole thing is ridiculous," I said angrily. "Just tell me what happened I need to know," I added.

"Sir, if I knew anymore, believe me, I would tell you, but we just don't know yet." The man said.

"Who are you?" I demanded.

The line on the other end went blank for a few seconds, all it seemed like an eternity after I finally got an answer.

"I'm detective Thomas with the federal investigation Bureau. And we're on the case to figure out what happened to your wife sir. And believe me, we will find out. We believe that it was in some sense an attempted homicide. Although we cannot be sure." He explained. "Some restaurant owner found your wife outside a bar in Brookland very injured and unconscious. Further then that, we do not know."

After hearing this, I didn't know what to think, the thought of what the man had just said almost made me feel physically ill in my stomach. How could this have happened? Why did this happen? All the while I was thinking about all these things, I realized I was still on the phone with this investigator. I quickly snapped back to consciousness and responded.

"Can I come see her?"

The voice on the other end became course and nervous. "Uh... no, fortunately not right now, she is in a delirium and needs some time to recover before she gets visitors. However, we will keep you updated on this situation. Thank you Reggie."

The phone then abruptly hung up before I could even answer to his last statement. I sat there, unable to react, or believe fully what I heard. You just don't really prepare for these types of things to happen. We all just assume that we are invincible, and nothing bad could ever happen to us. But they do.

A full month passed before I got any more information on the situation. And that little amount of information was still nowhere near enough to give me an idea of what was going on. It was now the New Years of 1980. The most eventful year of my life.

One late afternoon on a Sunday I was called down to the Denver County Police Station, and was told that they had some information to give me, as long as I gave my piece as well. I didn't know what this was supposed to mean, but I simply wanted to know what happened to my wife. One officer brought me into the station and I directed me to a man wearing a bright red suit. I had never seen anything like it before, So vibrant, and yet so unnatural. The man looked up at me, and instantly his expression turned to one of excitement.

"Yes, hello Reggie, I've been wanting to talk to you for a very long time." The man said, snarky in figure, and decently tall relative to everyone around him. He wore a crimson red suit, something of which made him stand out more than anything else. "You see we've been doing some research to find out what happened to your wife, and I think we found something that you might find interesting."

His thick New York accents indicated that he clearly was not from around the area.

"First of all, I would like to make it clear that your wife is all right. She's actually making quite a firm recovery," He said. "But, as you could probably tell, that is not what this is about," He concluded.

After this he directed me to a hallway on the right, that seemed to go down all the way to the end of the building. I followed the man, all the way down to the end of the hallway, which seemed to be miles long. It finally led to a dimly-lit auditor style room in which had one desk, along with two chairs sitting adjacent to each other. Once I stepped into the room I already noticed that there were a few other officers within, looking directly at me as if expecting something.

I soon began to realize what was going on.

"Now you see, Mister Green, I think you would fancy a seat, you have been walking for quite a while." He said in that same snarky tone.

"Can you just tell me what this is all about, why do you need me to answer your questions?" I asked.

"Of course, Mister Green. I would love to tell you what this is all about, but the simple rule is, that you must cooperate with us." the man answered. "Okay so let me see," He said as he reached his hands into an open file folder that was placed neatly on the desk. "Ah yes, I think this might be the one we're looking for." He said as he pulled a piece of paper out of the file. "Now Reggie, do you happen to know what Scopolamine is?" He asked politely.

"No not off the top of my head. Why?" I responded.

"Well, as it turns out, Scopolamine is a drug that is found common what South America, and most likely can only be purchased through use of the black market here in the states. However, it is certainly possible to obtain." As he started to fidget with the paper in his hand he continued. "And it just so happens that as of looking into

Jessie's packings, we found half a gram of this substance placed neatly next to her allergy medications." he continued.

"I am just simply perplexed, as she has revealed to us that you usually are the one who organizes her medications. She told us that you were the only one who could remember the right ones. Do you somehow know how your wife managed to get over a quarter gram of the substance in her system?" The man's tone was becoming harsher, and stern. I felt framed, and violated.

"Are you accusing me of trying to kill my own wife?"

The whole demeanor of the man was now beginning to anger me.

"Listen, Reg, don't take this too out of hand. As long as you answer our simple questions there will be nothing to worry about.

Now can you please just answer the question?" The man replied.

"I just came here to find out what happened to my wife, and now you're asking me if I tried to kill her? Can you at least stop being so mysterious and tell me your name?" I asked firmly.

"My name?" The man's grin widened. "I can assure you Reggie, my name certainly does not matter right now. What matters is you walking out of here either in handcuffs or with what you want to know." He said. "Now, can you please explain to us how you think this substance got into your wife's suitcase?"

I decided to simply not reply, as the accusation of me hurting my own wife was too ridiculous for me to even acknowledge. I sat there awkwardly watching as his snarky smile soon faded into a displeased frown.

"All you have to do is just answer the question. I don't even care if you answer incorrectly, just answer the question Hank, and you can walk out of here," he said after a while.

"You truly sicken me." I responded at once.

Instantly his frown turned into a pure look of boredom.

"Well, I think we're done here." The man got up and swiftly walked right past me and straight out the door. The door closed with a big hit. And I was soon left in the room with the simple mirror, which I should assume was a one-way window, and two security officers that were now approaching me. They told me to stand up, turn around put my hands behind my back, and then proceeded to tell me my Miranda Rights. It wasn't anything interesting to me, had been through this once when I was 15 when my friends and I ditched school day, the last day of eighth grade. However this time, was completely different, I was fully framed.

The next thing I knew, I was in the backseat of a sheriff's car. And that's all I remember. Only then could I recollect on the time I was tossed into the cold hard reality which was materialized into a prison cell. Nothing more than a bed, sink, and a door leading out only subjecting me to the sounds of anguished prisoners.

The day that I found out that she died, was the day that I realized just what type of situation I was in. It turned out, that she had suffered some type of relapse which had taken her into a coma and the doctors had to cut off the life support. And just like that, the one thing in this world that made me happy was gone, and along than that, I was accused of taking it away from myself. Only a few months went by until I was firmly greeted by my trial.

I had almost no warning and no way of even defending myself. I was alone. Only comforted by the legally assigned lawyer. Day and night we went over the testimonies and my own defense. The lawyer told me what was at steak, but it seemed that he cared more than I did. Many nights went by when I just lied awake thinking about the same story over and over again. I guess tonight was one of those nights. I remembered the rest of that trial.

As the judge fondled the papers and stared down to what seemed to be nothing, the courtroom became ever more silent. Both lawyers kept spouting out legal bogus that I could hardly understand, as I sat far in the right corner wearing my bright orange jumpsuit feeling betrayed by Society. All I got out of the whole thing was just simply acquisitions and arguments.

The judge eventually asked me to stand and profess my defense.

"Mister Green, do you have anything to say on your behalf at this time?" The judge asked.

Before answering I caught a glimpse of my lawyer eyeing me in a contradictory fashion. I knew, for my sake, it was in my best interest to not say anything. But I needed to.

"Yes, your honor" I squeezed out.

The lawyer now looked irritated at my decision.

"I would like to say that for all anything is worth, my wife was everything to me, and you can send me down the river all you would like, however, this will not stop the truth."

The jury looked astonished at this. My wife's family still anguished in their emotions sat back with almost no reaction. Their energy came off as being convinced along with shocked. At this to judge continued his verdict.

"Well then as the jury has made clear earlier, I believe we have come to a firm stance on the given punishment for this crime." The judge stated with a blank expression.

"The victim's family has stated earlier that everything Jessie did in her life was a reflection of her, and her death is the only thing contrary to that."

As the judge said those words I could hear sobbing coming from the corner of the Court of which my wife's family resided in.

"So forth by the jury's decree, the state approved execution as punishment of unlawful substance abuse, and first-degree murder shall be carried out."

As the judge said these final words the energy changed within the courtroom. The words slipped by me almost as a breeze of stale air. Packing little to no impact. But I could tell by my lawyer's reaction, he knew it was over. I fiddled with my chair a bit, still slow to realize what had just happened. My lawyer started fondling his papers organizing them in an abrupt way. There was only one thing that slipped out of his mouth after that.

"I'm sorry Reggie, but it's time for us to move on."

2. CELL BOUND

It's been almost two years now, I feel the same way I did that day. The day when I met that strange man in the red suit. And tomorrow will be the last day. This is the last chance I'll have to think about it. I had a habit of staying up until the early hours in my cell just thinking about these things.

The prison block was quieter than ever , but I knew there were many people other than me doing the same. It was just too perfect. I was as sure of it as sure as I am to be transferred to the death house tomorrow morning. Yeah, all this time sitting in the cell sure does give a man a lot to think about. A long time to plan his final words. The words that will go down in his history, the words that will go down in my history, the history that should not have taken place.

"But, never mind that,"

I thought to myself. This doesn't matter anymore.

I didn't grow up around religion, and I never really had a thing with Gods. But I knew that somewhere, now, Jessie was seeing this. She was seeing me hopefully the same way that I was seeing myself. I still loved her. I'm sure you would think a man in this position, only hours away from his own death would be scared, nervous, or sad. But I was none of these.

I didn't know what it was, but I knew that there wasn't anything to be sad over. Life goes just as it comes. And there's no way to control it I guess. As I tossed over my pillow, and lay rest on my right side facing the eerie dark prison Hall right outside the bars, I felt myself slowly drift away.

I awoke to a very harsh crackle on the prison bars. It took me a few seconds to gather myself, but once I did, I realized just what time it was.

"Okay Green, 8:30, rise and shine."

A familiar looking warden told me as he opened the prison door.

"Yep, we went over this before but legally I'm supposed to tell you what we're doing." The guard said hastily.

He gestured me towards the door, where I would soon see another guard approached with a pair of restraints with him. The officer mumbled something as he fixed my arms together, I couldn't determine what but I figured that transporting condemned prisoners over and over again for a job must take a toll on you after a while.

"Alright Green, so we're going to get you over there and then that's when you're going to get

your final phone call opportunity, understand?"
The warden asked.

"Yeah,"

I mumbled.

After what seemed to be a while of going through twists and turns of hallways we finally reached a pair of sliding glass doors which led straight to the outside. A few other men waited there for me, and I almost expected to see the man in the red suit again for some reason.

That vibrant red suit stuck with me for the longest time. I simply could not get that memory out of my head. The guard assisting me tossed me into the hands of two officers that led me into a prison van.

"Reggie... Uh, Green. Yes, he's one."

I heard one of the suited men say under his breath to the warden. They closed the door to the van with me inside. In the moment, I knew that it was the last time I would see sunshine. The inside of the van was dilapidated, and dull. No windows, no nothing.

Right before the van pulled away from the paved parking lot, I managed to hear one last line out of the warden's mouth.

"Don't bother letting the call go more than three minutes, ain't no one important enough that I reckon he's got to talk to."

It was a short but bumpy ride, and seemed to be less than 10 minutes. I knew this entire area, I had grown up around here when my parents weren't able to watch my brother and me. There was just one main Highway leading straight to Houston, and the other way went straight to Dallas. Definitely not much to see. I remembered playing in the thick forests at my grandparent's house during the winter. It was never cold.

I just thought of those times during the ride. I thought of one day in particular when my brother and I were out playing right outside my grandparent's house. I remembered getting lost and walking for almost an hour down the highway, meeting straight back to the house.

The highway always seemed to connect everything together. It was the whole world to me down there. When the doors were eventually opened, I couldn't see anything but a brick wall. This time there were no men coming to escort me out. It was just one police officer. Plain and simple. Bald head, and some swagger looking sunglasses. Nothing more than a gray generic suit with a bright star badge that I was familiar with.

Obviously some sort of certified sheriff of this County. His badge read officer Keith. He simply pointed towards the door and used his head as a gesture for me to exit. I had nothing to protest, so I did exactly as he ordered. The cold breeze was a little bit more apparent there, the sun was masqueraded by the clouds, which inevitably added to the droopy feeling.

Only now I began to feel scared, but not quite scared for myself, but scared for what was going to happen. What was going to happen in the future? It's hard for us humans to accept our end. Ends don't really register in the wiring of our minds. That's why whenever my parents would tell me a story, instead of mustering out the typical "the end", it would be something along the lines of 'to be continued', or 'to this day'.

I always enjoyed that.

"So you know what you're here for don't you Reggie?" Officer Keith asked me as I stumbled out of the van.

Before I could reply, I was forcefully escorted into the brick building by another guard that I can only assume was the driver of the van. He came almost out of nowhere, which was enough to give me quite a spook. As I was entering through some old decrepit doors, of which were manually opened by a key the officer fidgeted with for awhile, then a loud clunk was heard as it opened.

What I saw was just a simple grey room with a bench and a toilet adjacent to it. The door leading into the room had just a single small rectangular window, with wires tied together within it. Then a simple mailbox style opening within the iron door which from what I could assume was meant to transfer items into the room. The ground was made of some Stone material which made the room feel really cold.

As I made my way inside, the handcuffs on my wrists were removed by the warden behind me. Still wearing my jumpsuit, I was positioned into the room and sat down on the hard makeshift style bench, which I suppose was meant to be the bed. The second officer walked off before the door was closed behind me. Officer Keith gave me one last look of condolence before sliding the heavy iron door to a loud clunk sound as it was locked.

Often I heard chit-chat right outside of my cell from the many officers passing by examining me. This I suppose was the one thing that worsened in my anxiety. I myself was not scared of death, however, being a man sentenced to this, buy pure innate misfortune, I had nothing much to expect.

What should I have done? I felt all the pain and misery along with sadness within the walls of this dark confine. So many men before me going through this as I had. But why me? I tried to stop myself from playing out different scenarios in my head on what exactly I could have done to prevent it all.

But of course, I couldn't. All the while I hear mild footsteps walking down and up the hall right outside the thick iron door separating me. From time to time, I would see the outline of a face of an officer peeking in to observe me as protocol I suppose. One thing, there was one thing I just could not stop circling my mind around. Jessie... What would she be doing right now? What would she do, if she were...

My thoughts are bluntly interrupted by the sound of a scraping key against iron on the other side of one of these walls. Then the muffled sounds of yelling. Some scrap at the cafeteria, maybe? Or maybe it was just me. Hearing my own mind go completely insane. I don't remember much of what happened in between this time. At one point I had noticed a slight breeze underneath my half cut pant leg, which came straight from under the bench, or bed of which I was laying on. This was all followed by a slight electrical sound.

I hopped off the bed to confirm my theory of what it was. I leaned in to see a very small crevice which was followed by a lot more engraved on the tile wall. It was actually an air shaft, which I was particularly surprised at considering I had taken many courses in ventilation on and off through college.

The vent must have been some internal heating system. The fact that they would provide me with such comfort in my last few hours was actually quite amazing to me.

I leaned back on the cot style bed. One last thing fluttered through my mind. I got up once again and crouched down to see the same vent, with some heavily compacted screws, bolted the metal against the wall. I guess I was getting another crazy idea. Because I thought to myself if I could somehow unscrew those bolts from that metal shaft, I could have made it out of there. Considering that the vent led to the main heating system of course.

I kept wanting to call myself crazy over and over, but I just couldn't shake the idea that I could escape my own demise with a simple screwdriver. It was far too easy, part of me wanted to believe it was up. But if I had known anything about prisons, it was that they generally do not hand out screwdrivers to the inmates on a regular basis. I sat back, closed my eyes and dismissed it all.

"I will awake from this nightmare soon." I thought to myself.

My daze was cut short by the rattling of keys outside my door only minutes later. The mailbox entrance slid open and I was given a sheet of paper of which I could use to choose my morning meal. The paper said morning meal, I knew for a fact that it actually meant last meal.

I don't know why they couldn't just cut straight to the point, as the paper itself was dusty and clearly used. On it, I can make out several distinct food choices some of which I had actually never even heard of. It was fascinating to think about the many things one could choose to become his last dish, the idea of having one last sensation before utter nothingness was consuming to me. However, I did not hesitate to read to myself the what I thought was a relatively few amount of options.

Pork stew, salad, steak, cheeseburger french fries, all the rest. I had always been picky at what I eat since day one. Even my mother used to give me the typical non-sought after speech about how I was lucky to have anything at all. But in this sense, I had nothing to complain about. I just couldn't decide. After all, did it really matter? The only non-regulatory thing that was there was just a plain old stake. I peeled off the sticker for the option and dropped it through the crevice of the iron door slider. The paper was then taken from me by one of the guards outside the cell. Not even a small acknowledgment of my very existence was demonstrated.

It seemed as though I had been waiting for days. Sitting bluntly in the cold dark reality that I was in. The fact that over a year had gone by since I had been transferred to death row was almost unbelievable to me. I don't like to be scared. Even whenever I would hear a sound in the closet back when I was just a boy, so when I would take out the trash every tuesday night in our old backwoods cabin.

All the fear trapped in me, never got released. I would always tell myself; "I'm not a coward. I'm a man." Over and over again. But now was a different situation. Instead of telling myself this, I would only think about my wife. Day in, day out. In my cell, and out my cell. I would never blame her for my situation.

I had a hard time blaming anyone although it seemed like it would be easy. Easy to just hate the world for sealing your fate for a crime you didn't even commit. I just couldn't. The hours as it seemed that passed slowly as I waited for my last meal to appear at my door box were those that I used for these thoughts. Nothing more, nothing less.

I was starting to feel more and more comfortable as I waited. As weird as it may have seemed to feel anything more than forlorn in this scenario, something about it all just comforted me. The thought that it would all be over soon, and possibly, just maybe, see my beloved wife once more. Wherever that is.

However my intrinsic state of mind was abruptly interrupted once again by the intense sound of the iron latch to my cell door. This time they had opened the entire door to my surprise. A man that I didn't think I'd ever seen before wasn't shy to slide a box into the room. Swiftly with a hesitant nod to me, the door was slammed shut by the nearby guard, leaving me alone with the textureless black box sitting at my feet.

It obviously wasn't the most amazingly served dish, most likely made in the course of a few minutes. I reached out to it and lifted the side out to see the contents of the box. At first glance, it seemed to be exactly what you'd expect, a normally cooked medium rare steak. Just as I'd ordered.

As I began searching for the utensils I caught glance at a shiny object lodged at the back of the box. It was definitely reflecting the small amount of light offered in the room, and at the time of course was not much. I couldn't be bothered to just dig into the thing with my hands so I reached in, desiring for a simple fork to do the job.

Like they would be dumb enough to actually leave death row inmates a sharp instrument. And after all my study of the psychology of prisoners set to die, one thing was the most interesting to me. Not one man ever wanted to die by the hand of higher authority. Some type of hierarchical complex. So they would take advantage of any day to day material that they could find to end themselves with a statement of F-you sorta speak. I know they learned from that. They knew better now.

So what was the metallic object I was reaching for? As I had grabbed the object and brought it closer view I analyzed it and within seconds had become completely bewildered once again. It was a standard metal Allen wrench. But not the everyday kind, this was different in structure, size and appearance. I struggled to understand the meaning of what I was looking at.

I held the wrench in my hand a few moments longer perplexed at the sight. I glanced down at the box again, the former house of what was my last meal to see the sticky based note which lay aside from the steak. It had to have been directly beneath it, as I had not seen it prior. The note, in cursive writing, provided a simple; "USE THIS WISELY." The statement was there, in black in white.

I almost thought I was hallucinating the words before my very eyes. But no, there it was. Someone was actually trying to help me.

"Someone was working with me." I thought with internalized excitement.

Without a second thought, I at that point knew what I had to do. The only thing that could have been done. I once again crouched down towards the side of the cot to bring the air vent into view. Its position was awkward, to say the least.

And not one of which a man of my size could have apprehended easily. I squeezed myself further under the cot, firmly grasping the metallic gift I had received, further and further until I could reach out and grab the vent. I had no time to spare. Surely I'd reckon they'd be on their way to complete their task by then. It was far too late for any kind of hesitation.

The four screw holes wedged into the vent shaft were just barely shallow enough to get any decent leverage. As quietly and diligently as I could, I twisted the wrench in a clockwise manner. They were incredibly sturdy, yet also rusted.

Each quick twist I performed on the rustic bolts sent shivers down my spine. I felt the crisp air of freedom pass through the vent and on to my sweating face. The last bolt loosened with an abrupt CLANK sound. Not loud enough to attract attention, but loud enough to send me into a state of cringe. The bolt loosed further and slid out of the socket with no struggle. All four bolts now lied leisurely on the concrete floor next to me.

The vent was the last obstacle. There was almost no stable place to grip the thing. As crucial moments passed by so quickly, I ended up shoving my fingers into the crevice of the vent itself. With all the power I had to conceal the pain, one quick pull was enough to conquer it.

The vent was not as heavy as I thought. Only now was the air being blown against me at full force. A new smell had also manifested itself. Not a bad smell, more like the smell of dust and old furniture. Now was my chance.

Beyond what I could see passed the vent was nothing but blackness. The air also seemed to be getting exponentially hotter. I began to force myself through the opening.

My hands made contact with the bottom of the vent as I struggled to pull my body through. The edges were tough, but not sharp. The corner of the shaft seemed to provide just enough room for me to pull the rest of myself in. Now, I was surrounded by darkness. On my hands and knees.

The only and last foreseeable light coming from behind me. I began to carefully move forward through the shaft. Each forward motion created a slight echo through the material. I think it was at this point when my eyes began to adjust to my surroundings. Ahead of me, was about 50 or more so feet of the shaft.

I could make out a barely visible, yet very distinguishable opening. The air was traveling in my direction, so I carried on hoping for an inlet. Behind me, and around me... nothing but silence. Followed by an occasional distant buzzing sound coming from the opening in the shaft.

I kept pulling myself through, more and more of the shaft, as it got darker the further I went. There was no going back now. The opening was now right in front of me. Staring me dead in the face. Now the sound of running dripping pipes and the airshaft machine were clearly audible. I grabbed a hold of one of the pipes to thrust myself into the room.

The room itself was small but full of water up to the ankle, more and more of which was being delivered by some faulty pipeline.

At this moment I gained more vision. The room was illuminated to the slightest amount by an old rusted out light bulb in the corner protruding out of the brick wall. On the slide adjacent to it, appeared to be another shaft, but closer to the floor.

Low enough to where the water was slowly draining down it. I walked towards the drain pipe being careful not to knock my head on the ceiling, which couldn't have been more than a few inches above me. Clearly, this place hadn't been designed for anyone to be walking around in it. Or escaping from prison I suppose.

My path, however, was still clear to me, the drain pipe, I kneeled down to smell the foul sewage being treated through it.

"This is it, this is the one way road to a new life."

I said to myself eagerly.

The cold water at me feet seemed to be rising at the minute. More of it draining through the pipe I was facing. With one quick motion, I plunged myself into the pipe sliding down at dangerous speeds. The light behind me began to fade as I slid further into the abyss. Before I could process the situation, all but my sense of hearing and smell were depleted.

The smell grew worse as the speed slowed. The sound of rushing sewage against my jumpsuit was all I could hear. I felt my momentum weaken, the water slowed as I approached a what I thought was a lull in the pipe.

The water followed the direction of the pipe upwards to a break in the metal. A leaking stream was masquerading the light from outside. The hole, however, was further up the now slanted upwards pipe, making it almost impossible to achieve any kind of grasp to push myself up.

The water kept rushing stronger almost in wave-like patterns up the slope. All that was visible was the narrow slim of light protruding from the hole. Using a firm grip, I latched on to the sides of the pipe with all of the force I could use against my fingers, which I could only assume were pruned beyond what's normal.

The grooves inside of the narrow tube made it possible to pogo up to the opening. I got close enough to see the waters exit point. Almost none of it made it past the cracked opening, it was obvious the pipe itself had fallen into disrepair years before.

The sound of the rushing water falling beneath me was exhilarating to me. After searching for a decent view through the pipe wreckage, I discovered that it was wider than I had first thought. A waterfall of mixed water and sewage, impressive at that, flowed beneath me. Meanwhile,
I could only imagine the chaos occurring in the prison. I thought about being the only man to escape legally insured mortality, a legend. But more likely than not, a free man. Finally free physically and mentally.

I began to hurl myself into the plummeting water, falling many feet into a deep puddle accumulated by the leak. The pain of it was washed away by my emotions. It was a deep feeling of relief breathing in the fresh air for the first time in what seemed like an eternity.

I had known that by then, without a doubt the authorities would be endlessly and relentlessly combing these woods in their efforts. I had no time to spare for myself. I grabbed a nearby branch to make an incision in my jumpsuit, of which I used to tear off the remaining fragments of the drenched suit entirely.

I decided to follow the drain pipe on foot, hoping that it would have led me to some sort of civilization. However, I deviated from it to an extent to prevent an obvious path that could be tracked.

...

3. NEW BEGINNINGS

September 4th, 1985

Hello... so, I found this old journal booklet in the back of my old pickup truck close to town. God knows how it got there. So I guess I'll give myself some company writing in it for a while. I hiked along side of a path I found just out north of the pipe, I followed it and sure enough, it had lead to my family's old trailer park. My parents and I pitched our tent there from time to time on vacation periods. I don't even want to know how long I was out there for. The woods were thick and confusing. I'm tired, and now anguished, but I must move on. I think I have some oil for the truck, I can't be sure though.

September 5th, 1985

Ok, ok, I know me writing in this could be considered a waste of my valuable time, but I guess you could say I might need it later on. For my own future, if I even have one. Either way, I'm checking in again to talk about the truck. I managed to get it started, and surprisingly the thing ran smoothly for a while. 5 whole gallons of gas were left perched above a few barrels outside the camp. Definitely came in handy. I'm on the road as I write this. Haven't got a damn clue where I am as I have no gps, or roadmap.

I'm just winging it at this point. Not sure how long the fuel will hold out on this thing, maybe, I don't know a few dozen miles? Oh also, found some well fitting threads conveniently lying out to dry on one of the clotheslines outside the park. Not even that bad looking I might add. That's it for now me, I'll check back in when my life gets interesting again.

September 6th, 1985

Well, hi again me. If there is someone else reading this, I guess I'm in a magazine right now. Or back in prison, either one I suppose. I hope I'm alone though. I feel better out here like that. The nights seem to be getting colder, and I'm running out of options for food and water. It was times like a few hours ago when I really regretted not bringing along that steak they gave me. Nevertheless, I'm still out here in my truck perched out on some backwoods trail, leading to nowhere. Pitch black out here too, I've turned off the engine to conserve more gas. I think I'm going to have to ditch this rust bucket sooner or later, it seems to be ironically slowing me down in some way. I've decided I'm going to scavenge for water first thing tomorrow morning. I guess any good stream will do the trick.

September 9th, 1985

Alright so it's been a while since I wrote in here last, and surprisingly, nothing but the expected has occurred since then. I'm assuming the time here, but as I suspect, at a little past noon today the truck stalled and broke down. The gas monitor needle didn't point to anything, just dropped off the dashboard. Luckily though, I got the inspiration to start writing this as I just found a clearing to the woods in front of me. The truck behind me, lay empty and dead in the middle of this mountain road. I think I finally have the right equipment to move on forward on foot. A funny thing happened to me while I was writing this. I stumbled across another pond, one similar to what I found a few days ago. But this one was larger, and an outlet to a stream stretching from the south. This made me assume the better quality of water as well. The funny thing is literally right next to it was a large collection of grape vines dangling from a tree. This made the appearance that the grapes were hovering over the water bathed in a ray of sunshine. Like a holy grail had been discovered. I feel like I'm good on resources for now.

September 10th, 1985
I'm officially on my own out here. Nothing but my clothes, a pack that I use to carry my many grapes that I picked up, and you journal. I wonder why they call it a journal. Is it actually because you use it to

document a long journey? Thus the name? Whatever it is, it fuels my will to go on. It's not ambition however, it's a feeling of hope. Getting down to the reality of things, I'm going to take a guess here; I've been hiking for the past 10 miles. Maybe not. All I know is I have a long route ahead, and you're coming with me.

Update 2: The trees seem to be letting up a bit in front of me, I guess that could be a good sign. After all, I'm just out here aimlessly, feeling like a king, like a boss. Out here, I'm truly free. Yep, I might be losing my mind, or the fact that I just witnessed a moose up close for the first time. The elegance of it was overwhelming, like I had just transcended truly into the wild. It made eye contact with me for a few brief moments. Something about it connected with me before it scurried off into the brush. Almost like it could somehow understand me. Anyways, the sun's going down soon and I'm going to need a place to hang my hat. I'm writing this last sentence as I sit overlooking a small cliff facing the sunset. Feet dangling. I haven't felt this at peace in a long time. This area of land is famous for it, the Shoshone national wilderness sure lives up to its name. I might take a break from writing here for a while, I hope you don't mind.

September 19th, 1985

As I'm writing this I've officially run out of food and water. The time is... actually, I don't even know anymore. Early in the morning. I guess it's rude of me to not at least great you after about a week and a half of no healthy contact. Sorry about that. I have a lot of work I need to do in the coming hours so I'm going to try to make this summary quick. I finally made it down the opposite side of the mountain, and I've reached this clearing of wide open fields. However in the night, mostly last night, I set up camp at the foot of the forest. I had woken up from a dream I had, which was a remarkably strange dream at that. All I can describe it as, would be me running through the woods, with blaring sirens trailing me. And every move I made it got closer to me. When I had woke up, I had at first presumed that I had been awoken by my own subconscious after the dream had ended, but there was something else. I did hear sirens in the distance. But not police nor air sirens. No, not even loud enough to distinguish. But it sounded almost as radio static. Ambiguous in form. From that night on I have begun to develop this deep feeling of fear. Not normal fear, but an apprehension of the future. I still feel like I hear those faint sounds as I write this. At any rate, I need to continue my quest for more water, and determine the source of this eerie sensation.

There seems to be a lull in the forest a few hundred meters deeper in. I will venture there tomorrow.

......

The brush surrounding me was getting thicker and harder to see through. I had just started making my way from my camp, into the clearing ahead of me. There seemed to be a barely noticeable, yet identifiable path worn into the ground below me.

I followed it into what now appeared to be a blocked off opening within the trees. The blockage was tough but also weathered by branches and leaves. I began aimlessly digging through the brush until my hand was greeted with the sensation of wood. Not tree wood, or any type of bark.

Clean smooth wood, like the type they use in makeshift directional signs. Wood that seemed as if it had just been polished. I continued into the branches using all of the remaining strength that I hadn't already lost to the harsh thirst to pull away from the shrub in front of the sign. It was in clear view now. All of its glory, and size. Only being withheld by the dust coating it.

I wiped the ancient coating off the smooth oak texture, uncovering three legible words; "Shoshone Wilderness Reserve." The bold letters stood out to me as strange and confusing. I was unaware of any nature reserve in the area, or out here at all. I never graduated from geography class, but I knew I was reading an old unused, possible ancient sign. Maybe of old colonial native american times.

Although all of the sign's mystery baffled me, I began to realize that the path in front of me was now clear, along with the line of sight with the clearing. I also began to realize that the sirens were returning. I heard them close, near me somewhere. This time, however, they were much different. It was more to the likes of a high pitch radio feedback, on and off in the distance. More prevalent now than ever before. Along with the same uneasy feeling, I just could not place my finger on.

I felt it really getting to me that time. Almost allowing me to relive my dream, and all of the sensations I felt within it. As uncomfortable as I became due to the unconditional combination of dehydration and irritation to the noise, I continued into the clearing. Stumbling onto a log that had fallen in the correct way to provide a passage across what looked like a small ravine.

It was then that the sounds stopped. Completely and abruptly, coming to a halt. Due to my water deprived condition, I didn't spring myself up like I would usually do to avoid an awkward situation from escalating. I instead slowly regained my footing as my eyes caught glimpse of a black object sitting on the log in front of me. A handheld radio.

An old style communicator that was in good condition.

"Was someone out here with me?" I thought to myself.

"All this time, being followed?"

Once I fully gained a footing on the log, I took the effort of a stride forward to investigate the radio. But at a sudden SMACK sound... it all went black.

......

4. MOMENTO

I woke up in this place not knowing what had happened. Where was I? I've been in the middle of nowhere before but this time it was different. Did I crash? There wasn't anything around me. It's just the abundance of wilderness. It was surprisingly peaceful, yet at the same time unsettling because of the vast untouched forest around me. I had to get out.

My anxiety was acting up again. I didn't even remember my name. I started wandering around searching for answers. I had nothing with me, as if I was in some wild extremely vivid dream. I wanted to believe I was. The only thing I was wearing was bright blue cloths, along with some what seemed to be wood debris in my pocket.

"Is there someone around here... anyone!?" I yelled into the distance.

The vicinity was a vast seemingly endless anomaly of trees, grass and vivid mountains in the background that I could see. If I had remembered anything, from before what had happened, I knew I needed a settlement. A safe haven. Something. I didn't even want to think what creatures could be out there right now tracking my sent. For as all I knew, this was barren untouched wilderness. I tried once more.

"HELLO?. PLEASE!"
No answer.

I turned back to my original location to see something that started to flare my memory. It was the same hand radio that I had seen before on that log, laying right where my unconscious body had been. This time, someone was speaking through it.

I heard the faint words muffled out of the radio.

"Hello? Is there anyone out there? I really need to know."

The voice was that of a female, and I could tell from even at the distance I was, the distress in her voice matched mine.

"Look, I know you're probably confused right now. I was too."

The voice continued. I began to edge closer to the radio to get a better sense of who was speaking on the other side. Lackadaisical, and weary, I didn't know what to do at the moment. After a while of silence, I decided to respond to the unidentified caller.

Picking up the radio and holding the speak button, I responded with a simple;

"uh hi... where am I?"

A few seconds passed of silence before I had any response. Finally, something broke the silence.

"So you're out here too huh? I thought no one else would end up like me." She said. "My name's Luna."

"I'm Reg. Or Reggie." I responded.

"Oh like Reginald? Interesting name. I guess being in here for long enough makes anything different seem interesting." She stated.

"Yeah, well um, do you know where I am and what exactly is going on?" I asked anxiously.

"Well right now I'm assuming you're in the middle of nowhere, asking me a question I've wanted to know since God knows how long." She replied. "But if you made it out here, then you probably know your way around nature at least a bit." She concluded.

"I don't remember anything. And I need to find out how to get back home." My words started to seem frantic.

"Home? Out? There is no home, and definitely no way out." She said. "You'll understand more in time, but right now dude, you just gotta use a moment to take it all in."

The static on the other end grew dense. I knew this meant that she must have been calling from quite a distance.

"Take it in?" I asked. "What am I supposed to take in? And where are you even talking to me from? And how am I..." My questions slurred into the radio.

"Woah, hold on there buddy, one at a time." She responded.

"I'm out here too ok? Somewhere. What I know helped me at first was just admiring my surroundings. Just take it all in." The static on the radio stopped. I assumed this meant the other end was turned off.

It was so peaceful. Serene, and open. The weirdest thing about all of it was, there was no evidence of how I even got here. The sky was a bright blue. More than I had ever seen. The sun about midway to the horizon. I figured it had to be around 2ish in the afternoon.

I began to hear some slight sounds coming from behind. Brushing in the trees.

"HEY... Is there someone?"

I ran to the sight to see a series of broken down trees leaving nothing but burnt wood brushing against the leaves. I collected the fallen debris in hopes of being able to carve a safe haven into the ground for protection.

The burnt charcoal seemed surprising sharp. I plowed a piece into the ground. Multiple times. I did this near a tree so that the roots would support the underground portion from collapsing in.

By the time the sun had merged with the distant trees on the horizon, creating the most spectacular and real sunset I ever remember seeing, I had successfully created a hut. The dirt that was left out was incredibly heavy.

I was scared. I started thinking about bad things.

"What if I die here?""What if I never make it out?""Was there even a way out?"

All these things went through my head so fast, I almost didn't recognize the faint sound of footsteps outside. Very distant, but indeed there. This made my heart skip a beat. I had no light in the hole I had dug... no way of seeing, or defending. Outside was almost pitch dark now as the sounds seemed to come closer. Closer to the point that they were directly above me.

Each pound sent rubble from the dirt ceiling falling towards me. I had nothing to do. Nowhere to go. I waited for the sound of a roar or something to fill the small dirt room as my life slips away. But no... Nothing. I do not know how long I was sitting there listening to only the ringing in my ears. Too long. After what had seemed to be an hour of time, I somehow racked in the courage to stick my head outside. My eyes adjusted.

Besides the eerie silence, there was no sound and no creatures anywhere. The trees didn't even seem to move in the wind. I can only hope I had imagined the essence. Before I could let any more of the bad thoughts cross my mind, I gathered the remaining dirt left over from the digging and created a covering for the hole.

I spent the rest of the night thinking, I didn't rest my eyes once.

"What is this place?" I kept pointlessly asking myself.

I was pondering these things in the pitch black environment of my dirt hut when suddenly, I felt a slight buzzing sensation come from my side, accompanied by the familiar radio static. Fumbling for the scanner I must have been lying on, the same voice returned from before.

"So do you seriously not remember anything?" The voice asked.

"Not a damn thing. And I'm beginning to question my sanity." I replied.

"What did you say your name was again?" She asked.

"Reggie" I muffled.

"Well, *you remember that.* Just think about the positives for now. I guess you don't have much of a choice. I've been trying to make it out here in this wilderness for months now. All I had was the land around me and this walkie-talkie. Just like you. I almost feel, better knowing I'm not alone out here anymore." She said.

"None of this makes any sense." I said into the radio.

"I know, but hey, sometimes you have to make sense of things. Now maybe you should just lay low, and gather yourself for tonight." She said.

I tossed the radio on the dirt floor of the hole and sat back in a fetal position. I felt my old childlike fears returning to me. Not scared of the dark, but scared of the unknown in general. It wasn't even an hour later... when I heard the faint footsteps coming closer in the distance once more. Inhuman, and deliberate. Right before I closed my eyes the radio spoke to me once more. "Goodnight Reg."

5. DEAD MAN'S TRENCH

The first thing I remembered was the slight light of the day peeking over the top of the hole. The covering I had made last night must have collapsed. Things were starting to come back to me a bit. My name was Reggie, the last name was still a blur. Knowing my name again is almost like meeting myself.

I was startled at the fact that I no longer even knew who I was. Lots of dirt seemed to have collapsed when I passed out, as I was covered in some strong smelling grass and mud. I gathered myself up and climbed out of the gaping hole I had dug, remembering the handheld radio, I turned and began digging in the dirt looking for it.

I searched for a good three minutes before finally digging up the now filthy antenna of the radio. I climbed back up the dirt mound into the small clearing of green trees. The air was crisp that morning. "HELLO?" I tried again loudly. Nothing. One thing that was definitely off that caught my eye, was that there didn't seem to be any birds. Or any animals for that matter around.

I believe that one of the scariest situations one can be in is lost in a place completely unknown or unrecognizable. Nature at its greatest. I started walking in the direction of some larger trees I spotted in the distance. I imagined some sort of large pines.

The sky was bluer than I could ever imagine possible. Not that I even remembered that much of such. It was one of those "I just don't know what to think or do" situations.

As I moved closer towards the pine forest, I noticed the grass had gotten darker. Crisper. Everything about this wilderness was just, so unbelievable. The smell of pines filled the air as I moved closer to one massive tree that stood out to me. I noticed very odd marks on it. Some sort of claw marks. This unnerved me more than it should have. For the last time, I called out as loud as I could; "HELLO?? IS THERE, ANYONE, HERE!?"

As soon as I had, everything seemed to get even quieter. Even the ringing in my ears stopped. The smell was familiar.

I started to gather up some fallen pieces of wood and bark. Still disturbed by the huge scrapes left of the tree above.

They must have been at least a meter long. Three meters above the ground. I proceeded to gather the remaining wood on the ground of the forest, scraping off some of the pines. It was pointless to call out to anyone. My best guess is that I had been dropped off in the middle of nowhere, maybe because of a kidnapping? Maybe I'm a witness of something, and the authorities had to wipe my memories, and dispose of me.

What authorities?

Maybe this is a test.

Am I being monitored?

Watched?

My mind started to wander as I walked back from where I came from. If I could scrape anything from my now nonexistent memory, It was that in these situations, you need some refuge. Anything that could be out among the trees could be patiently waiting for their chance to close in. There are no laws in a world without people.

I took the sharpest piece of wood I had, and carved my name into the nearest tree. To mark my point. 'Reggie'

That's my name right? It's just Reggie? What else?

"Too bad the wildlife was not a good enough witness to tell me just what was going on." I spoke into the radio.

I didn't expect a response, or anything to respond. Knowing my only company for now would be Luna on the other end of the radio, I felt almost comfortable with it. Maybe she could help me figure out where I was or where I came from. A few moments passed of me investing the pine cone filled area before I got any response.

"Well aren't you just an early bird." The radio buzzed.

"What did I wake you or something?" I asked.

"What me? Nah, I hate sleeping in. Just thought you'd be a little more tired after that hike you made." She said.

I became perplexed at this.

"Wait hold up, how'd you know how I got here?" I asked in confusion.

"Well... yeah, I mean how else would you get here. This isn't exactly a campsite 10 miles outside a city Reg." She replied.

"Okay, so do you know what it is then?" I returned.

She sighed. "Been here long enough to know you just can't drive in or out." Her words sounded sincere, but I still wasn't satisfied.

"What stops you from leaving?" I asked. There was a slight pause before she replied.

"There's... there's a gate, but it's..." Before she could finish her sentence an irritating crackling sound overtook the radio. I heard sounds of metal on metal and what seemed like talking in the background. Whispering, but purposefully indeed. After a few seconds of this, it was back to pure static. Then nothing.

Confused and worried, I tried contacting Luna once more.

"He-hello? What happened?" I asked.

For a brief moment the radio was dominated by static. I started looking around my surroundings, as If I could find the answer to the disturbance somewhere near me. Of course, nothing but the silent pine trees amongst me.

"Did something happen over there?" Muttered Luna from the radio.

"Uh, no. I was gonna ask you that." I replied.

"Alright well, I'm not sure what's going on here but, I've had this speaker around for quite a while and never really got around to using it, ya know because of the whole alone thing. Maybe, it's just faulty. I don't know." I could tell Luna was growing a bit freaked out by the situation, and to say the least, I was too.

"Listen, Luna, I think right now I, or I guess we need to focus on getting through this. Whatever this is." I said.

"Yeah, you're probably right." She responded.

The line went blank again, cutting off the radio static. I didn't know where she was, or logically if her situation actually mirrored mine. It was at this time that I began to notice what I was wearing. Some tattered up jeans and an oddly new, and good quality looking T-shirt. And a type of shoe I don't recognize.

The cloths definitely were not used that much. "Is this a good sign?" I asked myself. "Does this say anything about my story?" No mirrors around to see myself. Not really much of anything. I placed the 10 pounds of wood I had gathered earlier on the ground near some soft pines. A fire would probably be easier to start here.

Just as I started lacing the wood with grass and leaves, I heard a particularly concerning sound in the distance. Near an apparent mountain ridge.

"What if I ha... " My thoughts were interrupted by the same startling screech. Louder now. I don't think I can recall any creature of that sort. But as it seemed to get closer it became far more recognizable. At this point, I was almost sure what it was. And sure enough, only a few seconds past before a wild looking dog came panting out of the brush. A wolf of some sort. It almost looked startled.

"Hey there little buddy." I said to it.

It didn't even seem to care that I was there. I took one step towards it and it growled looking intently at me. I guess it had just noticed I was there.

"It's okay, I don't know what's going on either."

If I remembered anything from school it was that animals like These, typically traveled in packs or in groups of some sort. It was all so strange to me why it was all alone. Maybe it was just as confused as me.

"Hey, I don't know what's going on, and even though you can't understand me, for some reason I have a feeling that you can." I said this just as the wolf, which I presumed became comfortable around my presence started to lie down and seem to relax.

It seemed really tired out, like it had been running from something. Or chasing. I lowered myself down to the base of a tree to rest for a bit myself. Only a few yards away from me, lay the wolf now tiresomely gazing off into the wilderness. I rested my back against the base of one of the largest trunk in the area.

The sun, which was now high in the sky was maskeraded by the colossal tree above me. I sat there for minutes on end, thinking to myself different outcomes to the situation I was in. The sweat on my forehead stagnated on my brows, I wiped it away with one swipe. As I did so, one name popped into my mind which I knew was important to me.

Jessie.

The name of my wife. I had a wife. I struggled to scrape more from my mind, to dig up more information on my spouse. Where she was, if she was alive, if she were even real. My mind fogged up before I could achieve more of the answers I wanted, almost like a timed arcade game level, I was locked out.

The coarse wood withstaining my back began to send painful sensations into me, and as my mind cleared further, a ray of blinding sunlight breached a gap through the leaves above me. I readjusted myself to avoid the strain, and caught the wolf again in my vision. Now, it was staring directly at me, with an emotion of some sort.

It felt as though the animal could empathize with me, on a mental level. It's hypnotizing gaze continued for a few moments, before the wolf sprang to its feet and darted off into the brush, the same way it had came. The refreshing shade around me began to diminish as the sunlight broke through more of the pine leaves.

It was an enlightening moment as I was once again bathed in soothing and bright sunlight. I decided that I had to return to gather wood, to prevent any type of helpless, cold conditions from plaguing me again that night. A fire would work perfectly. The wood remained where I left it last, separating me from the wolf, now covered in pine needles.

It wasn't much, but definitely enough to support a decent fire. I began to gather the wood back with me, holding the most amount possible in one trip. I passed through endless amounts of pines before finally coming across the bottom of a grassy knoll. Climbing it, I came to a clearing atop, with the hole I had created the previous night amidst.

I dumped the rest of the wood in the center of the clearing, to prevent the fire from spreading. The sun was still continually beating down on me from above. I felt myself pooling with sweat, yet still couldn't wait to enjoy the comforting heat of the fire in the cold night.

"Hey, you uh, you think that that I should make a fire or will that attract animals?" I asked into the radio. Luna responded hesitantly.

"Yeah sure, but, you're gonna need a place to kick back aren't you?"

"Uh yep, but uh, do you have any real estate out here? I don't see that many options." I said jokingly.

"Yeah, haha, no. What I meant was, I know a place for you to take shelter. At least for now." She replied.

"Oh yeah? Tell me."

"Alright well, the way I like to look at this place is through grids. Like I haven't mapped the place but I think I've developed a fully functioning navigation system. It'll help you find it." She said confidently.

"Okay, sounds good." I returned.

"Alright let's see, um, well I can only guess your currently located near the 10th parallel. And there's a small but decent cabin on the 20th parallel, so you might need some more hiking unfortunately."

"Woah wait, 10th parallel, 20, what?" I questioned.

"I don't want to get to far into it, trust me I've had a long time to figure this stuff out. I measure this place by parallels. Just like back in geometry class." She stated. "Do you even remember geometry class?" She asked.

"Not really. Thankfully."

"Okay well hear me out, the center of this reserve is well, the center, then we have the 10 kilometer mark, 20th, 30th, ya know."

"Uh, no, I don't really know. But I think I get you." I said.

"Good! That's all that matters. If your wondering where I would be in all this, I'd say oh, 80th. Maybe?"

"Ah so you're quite a bit out there." I responded. "Yeah, found this old beat up lodge, used some of it's supplies lying around, fixed the place up a bit, and now as snug as a bug."

I started walking back towards the pine meadow to gather the rest of the wood I had left behind.

"That sounds nice, but how exactly do you suppose I get to this 'cabin'" I asked tirelessly.

"Well Reg, can I call you Reg?" She asked.

"Yeah sure."

"Good cause it sounds better than Reggie, no offense." She confessed.

"Yeah, yep. No problem."

"Well Reg, I *don't* know exactly how to get there. Never been. But it's perched conveniently over a high ridge. I think it's kinda hard to miss." She said.

"So do I go now?" I asked.

"No! Definitely not. You're definitely gonna need some resources and a good night rest. I'll give you some directions to it tomorrow."

"Okay sounds good. I'll just have to deal with this luxurious hole until then." I said.

"Well you work with what you have." The radio cut out.

I picked up the remaining firewood, and began lugging it back to my camp. Up the grassy knoll, and to my refuge.

The fire I created was large, but calming, made with only a few minutes of agonizing stick rubbing. I sat at the edge of the flames absorbing the heat. The day grew low as soon as it came, and the ambition for tomorrow was certain.

Morning came as abruptly as the night. I didn't even remember going to sleep that night. There was a familiar scent in the air, I remembered smelling it the other day while picking up scraps of wood. Almost like a thick pine smell, like nothing else you would smell in a forest. I was lost. But there was no longer any time for complaining.

I have to now act on my misfortune if I want to survive. I got up and brushed all the leaves that had accumulated over me overnight, and began walking in the direction that I had seen the wolf come from. There was a difference this time, there were actually birds in the trees. And my clothes were just as torn up as before, but just a tad bit dirtier.

"What is the point of searching?" I asked no one.

What am I going to find? Snap! I had just stepped on something hard yet brittle. It almost had me tripping towards the ground. Before I could catch myself I saw what I stepped on. An assortment of bones, almost in perfect condition. A human skeleton? No, it can't be there are no other traces of activity here.

I picked up one of the bones to examine it. I noticed immediately that it was extremely light yet I could not break it. I didn't know where they could have come from. This was under a thick canopy of the leaves from the dense forest above me.

I could hardly see any clearings anywhere near me. The area near the bones seemed to be the only clear area of the forest. The only known one being further up the grassy knoll towards my camp. The only thing that caught my eye was a small point of sunlight coming from maybe, a few hundred meters in front of me. I collected a few of the bones and started towards the light. "There was almost no way through those trees." I thought to myself. "If I was going to get there, there's going to have been a more creative way of doing it."

I started climbing up the nearest branch and used the tree as a bridge across the huge ravine below me. I was unsure what measurements to use to demonstrate the size of the thing, but it would had to of been at least hundreds of meters deep. I kept dragging myself across the thick branch, almost as thick as a normal tree, but the whole way, felt like I was going to slip at any moment.

The sound of birds fluttering in my ears in all directions was almost as peaceful as it was distracting. Vines stretching from the branch all the way down into the abyss. I finally made it to the end, it had almost seemed like hours since I started. I stared back and examined the the cavern once more. The cavern was lengthy, more than it was wide. The trees around it formed a natural, and secure opening for what seemed like miles down in both directions. Along with vines stretching for possibly hundreds of feet below me, like something right out of a historic piece of art.

"Nature can build a bridge that boasts more impression than most men could say in a lifetime." I said gracefully into the radio.

"Good morning to you too!" Luna replied moments later.

"What are you reading a poem?"

"Nah, just thought I'd spice up my words a bit. I just found an absolutely amazing cavern, got me a bit emotional I guess."

This was a new way of traveling to me. The visible light was the now directly in front of me when I turned around. Water. The sound of it flooded the area. And I had just gotten used to the sound of the jungle and possible death.

"Yeah, that's dead man's trench. I've been around there once or twice. Probably not where you are, the thing goes forever." She said.

"Dead man's trench?" I asked.

"Ha, yup, just a name I came up with."

I looked back down to one of the bones I was still carrying. "

How'd you come up with the name? I mean you could have named it abyss of doom or, something." I stated.

"I remember being down there and seeing all these bones, like not human bones, but ya know, bones of something. Spread out all over the canyon. So, dead man's trench was just a way to label it."

Something about the name and the findings together gave me a deep eerie feeling. It just didn't seem natural. The continual sound of running water also caught my attention.

"Hey Luna, is there like a river near, 'dead man's trench?'" I asked.

"So if you turn around and walk like 15 steps, you'll see what I think you're hearing."

She did answer my question, I walked further down a naturally carved trail onto a rather large beach sitting at the foot of a massive lake. The lake was bordered by palm trees and massive waterfalls towards the opposite side of it. I presumed it they served as outlets to a river. And before I could think about it any further, I noticed in the corner of My eye, there it was. The wolf. Casually drinking from one of the streams breaking off from the lake.

So I thought it was but I wasn't entirely sure. I had no idea how many animals could have possibly been in the forest. Who knows if this was the same one. I decided to keep my distance this time and use the presumably fresh water to renourish myself. Whether it was safe to drink or not, I had no other options.

I drank a couple sips and splashed some on my face, before I turned around. It was now once again looking directly at me. Almost like a begging dog would at a thanksgiving dinner table. Like it wanted something. "Hey buddy!" I yelled. It kept staring at me. "Do you need something?" It just kept staring at me, like I was going to do something or steal something from it.

And once again, animals like these being all by themselves was typically unseen in nature.

"I..." I was cut off by the sound of shuffling behind me. Unorganized, and forced movement of sand, with a low but heavy thud each step. I almost didn't want to turn around, but I forced myself to. Having to see what I'd been trying to avoid this whole time. The thing, what I was now looking at, encountering, was the most bizarre creature I had ever witnessed, I didn't need a fully functioning memory to know that.

It was some sort of bear with missing fur and skin but not even as big or as bulky as a bear, almost like something an 11-year-old would think is hiding in their closet at night. It was looking right back at me. Or maybe it wasn't looking at me. I shifted to the side towards the lake just a few feet to see it was still staring in the same direction, directly at the wolf. They were both in charging position as if they were going to fight for something.

The wolf let out a loud cry. The creature ran off faster than I thought possible into the forest off the edge of the sand. Just as this happened, the birds seemed to return to their normal cheerful state. At that, the wolf got up from its position and continued to drink from the water. As if nothing had happened. I had no idea what to do or think in this situation, how to gather myself on what just happened. I decided to lie to Luna about what happened. She must have somehow heard the howl through the radio when I shifted to the side.

"Reg!? Are you okay? What was that sound?" She asked frantically.

"Uh, it was nothing, just some animal across the lake somewhere." I lied.

"C'mon Reg, I know the sound of a howl. You should probably, like get out of there. Just in case there's a pack nearby."

"Alright, alright. You're right."

I began making my way back to the entrance of the cavern, back to the ravine and towards the large tree which I had seemed to have lost. I needed that tree, it was the only bridge across the ravine. I dreaded what was down there. I for some reason, had a striking feeling of my childhood fear, the unknown. That's probably any humans fear. What was down in the mists of that dark and cloudy ravine is something that I particularly didn't want to find out.

The sandy shores of the lake seemed to hold one more secret. As I spotted a broken palm tree just a few meters in the distance. I ran over to it, and started to investigate. I didn't at all know what I had just seen but whatever it was was probably strong enough to make major damage, possibly collapse a tree like the one I spotted. The weirdest thing about the creature was it didn't make any sound. Like any normal animal would. As it charged off, the scariest thing that was brought to my attention, was that it acted almost creepily like a human.

Assuming the damage to the palm tree ahead of me was caused by said creature, whatever it was, it was kind enough to leave me some coconuts. I gathered them up, washed them in the stream for a few seconds, and then carried on into the forest in front of me. Almost instantaneously the crest of dead man's trench was met at my feet. Hundreds of feet below me was the unknown.

The only thing blocking it out, what is the natural sounds of the surrounding creatures. Birds, some of which I had never heard of before. Some squirrels possibly, and maybe even a few species of amphibians. "Where was that bloody bridge?" I asked myself furiously. I looked both ways, each trench was vast, they seemed to go for miles without any sort of way across.

"So, you feeling up to those directions that I promised you yesterday?" Luna said over the radio as my frustration heightened.

"Directions to what?" I replied.

"The 20th parallel dummy. You feeling up to it?" She said playfully.

I continued to search down the length of the endless trench for a possible way over.

"Yeah well, the only directions I need are over this trench. I think I lost the way in." I added.

"Oh, that's, kinda bad. Um, there should be a land bridge somewhere."

"Well there's not." I replied angrily.

"Okay, calm down, these things happen sometimes alright Reg? Just breathe, and think it through. There's a whole lot of misfortune out here. You need to work with it." She said.

I scanned my eyes around the area a last time to confirm my stranded state.

"I'm stuck here forever now at this lake with that thing?"

I questioned myself.

This was going to be hell.

I stared off into the distance, for some reason hoping to see the bridge that I had traveled across. Only to drift my eyes down a bit to see it on the ridge of the ravine snapped in half. Two halves stretching down into the darkness and fogginess of the cavern. It was gone. Whatever the thing was that I had seen probably used it to get back from where it came from.

One tree specifically stood out to me. For some reason, the way that it was angled, gave me the feeling that it was not natural. I jogged over to it, a bit downhill, And investigated the trunk of it. Some part of it seemed way older than all the other trees surrounding it, Like it had been untouched but yet damaged.

When I crossed the backside of it I had noticed something carved along the side of it, covered with a huge layer of dust. I put my hand out to wipe it off and the first thing that I noticed was writing. Carving into the side of a wooden plank, large and bulky hitched against the tree. I dusted it off for a good minute until I could read the almost illegible writing.

The first words I could make out... "To anyone who witnesses this humble time capsule, may peace be with you." I proceeded to wipe off the rest the dust, to uncover the rest of the statement. It was written in almost half English, and half of some other language I had never seen before. Nevertheless, I could see it as being familiar, somewhat resembling native writing and dialect. This is part of the legible statement that I could understand.

"Disaster has met our feet. We will not make it this time. Whatever they will do to us does not matter, the only thing that matters now, is our memory." And then the last part... "Austin, 1803."

"1803?"

"Was that some sort of date? What does this even mean, and who is Austin?"

My mind began to race, but I managed to control myself. I hadn't been the only one there.

"Hey, you know there's a sign down here by the trench. Says something about 1803." I talked into the radio. As I proceeded around the dilapidated tree, I got a response from Luna.

"A sign, like what a *sign sign*?" She asked.

"Like a piece of wood with carved initials into it, signed by some guy named Austin in 1803."

"Huh, interesting. Never came across it. You making any progress on that trench crossing either?"

I had almost forgotten the fact of my stranded condition. The trench, now seemed as if it were taunting me, urging me to challenge it.

"Uh yeah you're right, I'm working on it." I said to the radio.

Giving one last glance at the peculiar wooden plank, I started back into the forest to attempt the dead man's trench again. It seemed like only mere feet before I was met with the rocky edge of the dark chasm. It did intimidate me I will admit, however, the battle was not won yet. I edged sideways towards the snapped hollowed out tree that I used to cross initially. The tree, still dangling by the roots lodged deep within the rock, stretched down into the darkness. 30 or more feet ahead of me, the other half, mirroring it. The birds and animals within the ravine seemed to hush themselves at this moment.

My feet seemed dangerously close to the edge as I was beginning to run out of space. I began noticing what was lacing the walls of the ravine. Countless dozens of vines stretched as far up as some of the trees above me, hugging the sides of the rock down to the bottom. I took a hold of one stretching my arm out along the narrow amount of space between the trench and the tree line. It seemed firm and sturdy enough to carry my weight without a doubt.

I was apprehensive of my current idea, but I had no other choice. With one leap of faith, I latched myself on to the vine. I felt myself slipping before my foot met a rock sticking out the side of the chasm. The vine was long. I thought, and hoped long enough to get me across. The protrusion that I was fastened on gave me a chance to launch myself into the side of the snapped tree.

At this point, I could see the bottom of the ravine, a dark pit with a running stream of water below me. With all my strength, I lugged myself up the slippery bark of the fallen tree using only some snapped branches above me like monkey bars. I eventually made it to the top, exhausted, and heart racing. I stood at the edge of the trench opposite of where I'd just been, masking in my accomplishment. The beach, the waterfalls, and the sign, now cut off from my reach. I was most certainly not going to try to perform that stunt again.

"Okay, I made it over dead man's trench." I told Luna.

"Well, you've successfully done something I've actually never done. Congratulations Reg!" She replied in a joyful tone.

"I also think I just invented a new beach, dead man's beach which is now fully impossible to get to." I said.

"Sounds good to me." She said as I began walking back into the forest. My memory, although plaguing me with its absence was slowly recovering. I felt myself begin to pick up more and more of who I was, my wife, my life before this. It seemed as though more came back to me by the hour.

The hike back to my camp was primarily uphill, and through dense trees and brush. I had marked my way using certain trees as mementos to where I had come from. I came to a clearing halfway up the extent of the hill where the trees seemed to break off into a small field. The sunlight now gave its full force to me. As I was bathed in the light, something within me clicked and more of my memory came to me.

My wife was dead. She died of unknown circumstances, and I was blamed. Blamed for all of it, and more, I began to cross the field and the grass got taller the further the went. Once again, my mind began to close up again, leaving me with these new realized truths. Had I killed my wife, Jessie? I remembered her name clearly now. I remembered everything about her, and us, what we planned together. I couldn't have killed her. It wasn't true.

The grass was a bright orange color as the sun dropped closer to the tree line. I couldn't have been far from my camp. I carried on from the field further uphill. Once I did reach my camp five minutes of hiking later, I saw what was left of it at least. The camp itself was completely different than when I was there last. All of the firewood had been taken, some thrown around, and the rest vanished.

My shelter and stronghold dug unprofessionally into the ground, now was nothing but collapsed dirt. I walked closer to the scene, seeing that the grass itself was torn in places. Large chunks ripped out and thrown about. There were no footprints, however, after savaging the area expecting to trace a paw print, alas, nothing. No signs of any deliberate cause or pieces of evidence.

"Hey, Luna?" I felt my voice tremble as I mumbled into the radio. I was truly panicked.

"Yup, what's going on?"

"I need those directions to this 20th parallel thing now, my camp has been completely destroyed." I was basically yelling into the receiver at this point.

"What do you mean destroyed!?" She replied.

"I mean literally everything is torn up, and all my firewood is gone, everything is trashed. It looks like a goddamn tornado hit the place!" I now stood over a large chunk of the ground that had been entirely ripped out. "What do you think could have done this?!" I yelled.

"I, I don't... I really just don't know."

"You're the one who's been out here for so long, how could you not know?" I asked.

"I don't know! Okay, Reggie. I don't know what's out there. This is the great outdoors, anything can come and go as they please. I just don't know."

The reception of the radio began to fade. The gate. I remembered what she had begun to tell me before.

"What's the whole 'gate' thing about?" I asked. There was a moment's hesitation.

"The gate... it's uh, more like a barrier. A large fence surrounding the area. I never..." The radio began to cut out entirely at this point. Pure static now filled my ears. A few seconds went by when the signal cleared up. "But it's definitely there. Out there just a bit farther than where I am." She finished.

"Why didn't you tell me this before?" I asked impatiently.

"I don't know much about it. I never did go there, but I've seen it." She said. "It keeps me from leaving. Whatever it's true purpose is, it keeps us from leaving."

Now, I was beginning to piece it all together, all of what I knew. There was a barrier, an enclosure, that Luna and I were trapped in. I was also beginning to have a feeling arise in me that someone, somewhere did not want us, more particularly me to know about it. However, this piece of knowledge did not make me feel safer, or in anyway alright with my situation.

I felt panicked, and in danger. The radio in my hand was now overcome with white noise and interference. This time I knew it wasn't a malfunction. The signal was being blocked. I knew that there was no point trying to regain contact with her, the radio itself was clearly being manipulated. The thought made me feel even worse, and more confused about what was going on in a general sense.

The radio, oddly enough, had a clip built into the back end of it, that came to good use. I decided to strap it to the side of my pants until the interference had cleared up a bit. Another thought occurred to me, this so called 20th parallel, and the refuge it supposedly provided. Whatever, and wherever it may be, I knew I was in dire need of direction. I started to examine the mess around me, as I had seen before, firewood, and grass had been ripped away like wallpaper, thrown about everywhere.

However, I began to notice what arguably was a more disturbing sight behind all of it. Surrounding me, and the robust wreckage, all of the trees had been torn into and scratched, leaving similar marks to what I could recall finding in the pine forest. As I looked closer at one of them, I realized they were the exact same, in size and shape.

Every single tree serving as a boundary to the open clearing had gotten these horrendous marks inscribed on them. Like whatever had done this, was in a sense marking its territory. Declaring its dominance. I began to hear the mumbling of Luna's voice over the radio again. Without hesitation, I grabbed it and spoke.

"Hello, can you hear me? I need to get to that 20th parallel thing now."

"Are you sure you want to do that? I mean it's past noon and..."

"Yes! Yes, I'm sure. I need to get there as fast as possible." I cut her off, Probably at my most panicked state yet.

"Okay, I'll get you there. But know that you've got a long road ahead of you." She responded.

I began to gather some of the of the scattered firewood as a resource. I was not taking any consideration of the time as I got a callback.

"What are you doing?" She asked as I reached for another piece of the burnt material.

"I'm not taking any chances around here anymore. I need some resources if I'm gonna make it out here." I replied.

"No, no no, trust me. Where you're going has everything you'll ever need. There's literally just enough daylight left to make it there as it is. There's a trailhead a little bit off the side of that lake you saw earlier, it'll take you there."

I took a moment to think about the proposition. As I did, I dropped the wood shards and took her word.

"Okay, you win. I'll head there right now."

"Please hurry, you don't wanna be out there alone after dusk." She said worryingly.

"This trailhead, what's it for? I asked.

"For now, it's for you to use and not get killed out there partner."

...

6. FOLLOWED

The forest was dark and in my point of view menacing, considering what disturbing events had taken place. The only sense of any type of direction I had was the bland amount of instruction I was given by Luna. The trailhead had to begin somewhere out here, adjacent to the lake and dead man's trench. That is what Luna had told me overall.

I began to realize that I was beginning to actually put full trust into someone who I'd still never seen in person before. I had never had an encounter with the mysterious voice on the other end of the radio, not once. At the thought of it, so many more began to flutter my mind. So many different possibilities, some of which I didn't even feel comfortable sustaining.

If it were all set up, a trap, anything worse, than what was I walking into? I was still walking through the thickening trees as the environment around me seemed to get darker. More untamed. It looked almost the exact opposite of what you'd expect of a trailhead. I shook the unkempt thoughts from my mind in an effort to regain my focus. If there truly was a trailhead out there, I needed to find it, as the time was against my efforts.

The one thing that I noticed as a common pattern in this wilderness was apparent to me. The animals and wildlife seemed to be on and off in their existence. I would at times constantly feel surrounded by even the tiniest of living things, and suddenly, they would be gone. All traces of life seem to be vacant from the wilderness entirely. I did notice this occurring any time that, 'thing' crossed my path. That bizarre ungodly creature that more likely than not, was also responsible for the havoc back at my camp. However as I continued my venture through the forest, in an attempt to seek out this trailhead, I had a different feeling. It did feel like there were presences no doubt about it, but not natural presences.

I felt eyes on me. Not that of an animal, or creature, but the feeling of eyes analyzing you. Watching you. Usually only humans are capable doing. But I knew there wasn't anyone out there, it just, couldn't be anyone. The feeling still stayed at the tip of my tongue as I continued on. Surely enough, and to my own surprise, I reached an opening in the trees to what seemed to be a long carved out path. Wide and highlighted. I guess I could understand now why Luna didn't particularly feel the need to give me in depth directions.

My mouth was parched at this point. It must had been a solid 12 plus hours since I had consumed any liquid, not to mention the hissy fit my stomach was beginning to pull. I could only hope staring down the path of the curved trail, a glimpse of hope may of lied ahead. Not knowing how much longer my conscious being could last in these conditions, I began down the tail with the best hopes.

The sun, now close to the treetops taunted me. Only relieving me of the unsettling feelings I experienced off the grid. I truly felt alone to my thoughts. And comforted by the semi-presence of another person, strapped to the side of me. I smiled and continued down the trail.

...

I awoke to a wet sensation on my cheek. My eyes, practically felt glued shut, along with my mouth due to the dehydration. I jerked awake as I gained sentience. This must have given the animal right next to me quite a surprise as it jolted back about 2 feet. It whimpered and cried at my rushed awakening.

I slowly pulled myself up, feeling the lack of energy within me and wiped the course dirt from the side of my face I'd passed out on. I assessed my situation, and realized I had fainted dead on the trail. My mind and memory to how far I had traveled were vacant. I found myself turning to the startled animal that had awoken me. To my disbelief, it was the wolf once again. The same wolf I had seen many times, and now before me it stood staring, almost with a dog like orra.

I didn't know what to think or do in that situation. Had it been following me? I thought to myself. Surly a normal animal of this nature wouldn't give the slightest amount of interest towards human activity. This wolf however, seemed to be lured by me, as if guiding me. I must had walked for miles, as the area around me seemed completely unfamiliar. The trail also was narrower, and barely made it through some of the brush at places. The wolf remained still, with a peculiarly wagging tail, something I'd never imagine untamed animals would do. It stood there like it was waiting for me to do something.

"What should I do?" I asked the wolf.

It continued to stare at me passionately as I sat back down on the trail floor.

"I'm not sure if I'm going to make it boy." I said to it feeling defeated.

It's tail stopped wagging and the wolf brought itself to a lying position. If it had been following me it surly had to be as tired and restless. The thirst seriously began to set in when I layed back down. I stared at the open cloudless sky, streaked with orange color as the sun sunk deeper towards the horizon. I began to feel my own mortality manifest itself in that moment. I knew death was upon me.

In what I thought could have been my final thoughts, I remembered my cell, and the jail, and the sentence I had been given. I remembered the escape, the vent, the pipe, all of it. I even began to remember the man. The man in the red suit. He stood out the most to me, as the man who I saw so vividly in my mind now. I knew I could at least die satisfied that it was all clear.

"I think I should name you. Malos." I said to the wolf as my vision faded.

Right as I felt myself slipping my body suddenly jerked into motion, I felt my radio going off like crazy. Within a second, what seemed like my dying breath turned into a surge of energy from deep within me.

I had a chance. I grabbed the radio to stop the infernal vibrations. With radio in hand I pushed myself up from the dirt ground of the trail and without a moment's hesitation took off further down it. I noticed the wolf had also vanished, but my main concern was getting to the 20th parallel, the very place I had started for.

Jogging now uphill the jagged path with the last pinch of energy I had left, I began to see the trees distance themselves on either side of me. I slowed down and realized I was on a ridge, the path leading up to it. Both sides of the path now gave a wide open view of the surrounding area. Out of breath, and at the brink of exhaustion, I fixated on the rest of the path leading further up the ridge. The rocky mountainside lay at the furthest point from what I could see was a sheer cliff overlooking the wilderness. Atop of it, an astonishing sight, that I at first dismissed as only a mirage. A large wooden cabin that was perched overlooking the cliff. After confirming my eyesight, I knew It was indeed what I had come for. This was the 20th parallel.

The dirt path had now turned to gravel and lead up to the perched safe house. I was ecstatic at the sight of it, I felt the lingering feeling of hopelessness that had previously been covering me diminish. I began to make my way up the ratchet and twisty ridge path to the cabin. From what I could see of it at a distance, it appeared to be in decent condition despite its old appearance. The house was accompanied by a few small pine trees huddled about towards the end of the ridge.

Just observing the view on both sides of me was enough to know the altitude was monumental.

The house atop the rock cliff was perched definitely over a few hundred feet above the treetops, giving a clear view to another mountain range in the distance. For the most part aside from that, the entirety of the area was nearly flat. Seeing that the sun had nearly sunken completely into the tree covered horizon, I thought that I should have the common decency to make my radio companion aware that I wasn't dead.

"Hey... Luna, I, think I made it to the 20th parallel, it's supposed to this ridge right?" I asked and waited patiently for an answer. However after a straight two minutes of waiting, I began to get worried. "Hey Luna? Are you there?" I tried my luck again. Still after a minute or two of waiting, no answer. Not even the radio static seemed to kick in. Everything was dead silent, in that moment. I had been stuck in my own exhilaration to even realize it until then.

There was no sound. I was almost familiar with the phenomenon after all the previous experiences, it mainly didn't bother me at all anymore. There was simply an extremely disturbing feeling that came to me when things went silent. In a normal situation silence is great and definitely well needed, however, no matter how much I tried to shake it, the silence that would occur occasionally in those woods always gave me an unsettling feeling. I wandered over to the back side of the wooden lodge in search of an entrance. There was one, a small and well hidden oak door built into the frame of the thing. I tried the door but it wouldn't budge, sealed rather than locked.

The door itself had felt as if it hadn't been used in centuries. Each push I delivered to it sent a harsh shriek out of the wood. Tired, and frustrated, once more I spoke mindlessly into the radio.

"Hello Luna, please. Anyone!?"

My attempts seemed fruitless. I leaned up against the wooden door as I watched the remainder of the sun disappear into the vast nothingness of nature. The sky, once a vivid blue, now a dull twilight. Speckles of stars began to break through. I dropped the radio on the ground in anger.

"Had I really gone all this way, just for this?" I said aloud to myself.

I didn't feel like I even had enough time to enjoy my last sunset. The silence was interrupted by more of the abrupt shrieking. As I noticed it, I also felt myself slipping, but my feet were sternly fastened to the ground. Before I could register what was happening, in one quick motion my body swung downwards with the collapsing door I had been leaning on. I hit the ground hard into a spurred up cloud of dust. The door was not a door, but a simple wooden plank fastened into the door frame. It had burst into pieces on impact with the ground. As for me, the room I was now in was dark, only illuminated by the entrance I had just made for myself.

As my eyes adjusted though, I began to realize my surroundings. The cabin was far from empty despite what I had assumed. From my perspective, it looked like an entire well kept living quarters. The dust and debris on the ground supposed that it had been quite a while since any type of contact with this place had been made. Picking myself up from the rubble, I noticed more light coming from the far end of the cabin.

There were windows all around one end of the room. The break in the trees near them provided a view over the cliff and down the trail I had come from. Assorted next to the main windows, was a bed, stretched out in a cot-like style, and a table along with chairs and an open envelope. The table, which was well equipped with drawers provided a pair of black binoculars hanging from the strap. I couldn't stop wondering how the place was in such a remarkably good condition. Aside from the old wood and decrepit plank I had collapsed into, the cabin itself almost appeared as if it had just been cleaned.

I was bewildered at the scene. The next thing that stole my attention was the half ripped envelope that had been placed on the desk. I grabbed it, and inspected it. I could determine it wasn't any ordinary envelope I had seen before, although my improving memory was still not perfect. The only thing jammed inside of it, a journal, and freshly sharpened pencil.

It had been beaten up a bit, the hinges of the journal exposed and ripped. I scanned through some of the pages, looking for any possible clues of whom it belonged to. After only a few seconds of it, I practically gasped out loud at my discovery. The journal was mine. The very same journal that I had used with me on my venture through all this yes, it was all coming back to me. All of the transcripts of my journey were clearly written in my handwriting. I could feel the shocked expression on my face worsen when I noticed a sticky note attached to the back page.

"For Reginald" it said in plain writing.

At this point, I knew something wasn't right. The whole situation seemed off from the beginning. The feeling of being followed mixed in with the anxiety I had dealt with began to intensify. Surprisingly though, I was less confused than I thought I should have been. The fact that I used the journal through my time wondering the forest, only to end up here, and then incidentally end up with the same journal again made another piece to the puzzle. Someone, somewhere was testing me. Not any sooner did I remember the radio still laying outside the cabin.

I went to retrieve it when I realized the static was back on, blasting through the receiver.

"Hello, is there anyone there for like the 50th time?"

I asked as I picked it up. This time, it took a few seconds but I did get a response.

"Helllooo sunshine, so I reckon you made it to the 20th huh?" Luna responded sounding exceptionally cheerful.

"Uh yeah I did, where were you? I'm actually kinda dying up here you know."

"Oh I was just out fishing." She said.

"Fishing?" I questioned. "You just go fishing randomly?"

"Yup. Well, only on days like this when it's pretty good conditions, all of them are easy to catch. The hike on its own is worth it I'd say. You should try it sometime." She responded.

"Yeah, I should. Aye, um, does their happen to be any like, water around the 20th parallel? So I don't, die and stuff." I asked bluntly.

"Ha, you're gonna have quite a nice surprise up there. Check around back of the place, there should be something that'll solve your problem." She replied.

As she instructed, I made my way around the cabin through a dense patch of pines. Sure enough, perched against the house, was a water pump. An entire old style filter along with it.

"Make sure you take it easy with it though, not exactly healthy to drink too much at once." Luna said.

But I couldn't resist the temptation of taking it easy. Without any second thought, I started gulping down from the water faucet on the pump. The water was ice cold, refreshing, and had a slight but noticeable mineral taste to it. However much my body demanded differently, I heeded the advice from Luna to not intoxicate myself. The pump was another feature that baffled me on the condition the place was in.

"Hey, you ever go up to this place often?" I asked.

"Nope. Only once. I made it up there and used that pump to refill my jug and I was on my way."

"Why didn't you just take this place as a refuge, I mean there's quite a decent show of resources in the cabin at least." I replied. There was a moment's pause.

"What do you mean?" She replied sounding sincerely confused.

"Well, there's a bed in there, a table, hell, there's even some binoculars just hanging." I responded.

"Reggie I was there no more than two weeks ago, and there was nothing there. It was just an old empty shack with a water pump."

This statement really got to me. The fact that my intuition of how recent the place had seemed arranged was correct, made me question myself. I walked back to the front of the cabin towards the plowed in door. Sticking my head in through the dark and soothing room confirmed my sanity. The interior seemed so recently renovated, the wood around it seemed out of date in comparison.

"Hello? Reg? What do you see?" The radio chirped.

"There's brand new things in here, some of which doesn't even seem touched at all." I replied.

"Okay, well if that's not the creepiest thing I have no clue what is."

"Do you think someone put it here?" I asked.

"I don't know Reg. I really don't know." She seemed genuinely just as confused as I was. My attention was drawn to the journal once more, still laying on the table. I motioned towards it and took a seat on the single chair facing the window.

Looking down on it, I scanned through my past writings, all of my long journey, documented in front of me.

What I had not yet remembered about my experiences in the long arm of the law became real to me.

My mind was still glued to the sticky note I had found. It on its own made the whole situation I was in feel more controlled and formulated. Looking out the window, I realized that the last hint of sunlight had vanished from the sky, now leaving behind the dark sea of trees. I was in complete darkness, only due to the time I had spent adjusting my eyes could I even read the passages of my journal. The radio, sat silently next to me. Before I could gesture to it, Luna started talking.

"I got a fire going outside my camp, you might be able to see it from up there."

I grabbed the radio and made it out of the cabin, now once again overlooking the dark landscape.

"Okay, um, which direction are you in?" I asked.

"Just look around, you'll find it." She replied.

I scanned the horizon for a good minute looking for any indication of a campfire. I searched tens of miles in all directions until my eyes pointed out a very faint orange light in the distance. It was almost impossible to see without squinting.

"I think I see it!" I told Luna.

"Yeah, it's not like you're exactly playing where's Waldo out here. But that's me, way out at the 80th parallel." At this point, I remembered the binoculars that I found hanging off the table. I marked my spot on the horizon and ran back into the house to find them. They were also in an unrealistically good condition like they'd just come from the factory. Coming back to the spot I just had, I searched the area again with the binoculars. Sure enough, I once again found the orange dot, illuminating from a clear patch in the open forest. It was definitely her camp.

"I wish I could go down there and finally meet you in person." I said.

"Yeah well it's definitely too late for that now, you most likely wouldn't wanna be out there at night all alone. I think you've had enough experience with that for a while eh?"

"Yeah" I responded.

The orange glow intensified through my binoculars.

"Hey well if you ever do make it down here one day, I got a lot of extra tequila so... yeah."

"W-wait what? How exactly did you get that?" I asked.

"When you're out here long enough, you find a lot of weird things believe me. Don't even ask how I have three books of Harry Potter." She exclaimed.

"Three... oh, okay, won't even ask." I replied.

"Yup you'll probably be here awhile so I only hope you're comfortable up there."

I turned my gaze back to the now pitch black cabin behind me.

"Hope so too." I said to the radio.

...

7. NEW LIFE

Day 1

Hi, so I decided that I would pay my good ol friend a visit. Hello journal. So, where do I begin? I guess I'll start with the fact that I surprisingly slept like a rock last night. Not sure how I managed to make myself so comfortable here so quickly but, I ain't gonna fight it. As for now, this is my new home I guess, so might as well make the best of it. I hit a jackpot on the whole water situation, today I'm going to have to attempt to find some food, somewhere. I do however feel unconditioned to leave this place now. Haven't got a call from Luna yet today, I think I'll radio in and tell her my plan.

Day 2

So I was wondering around the place earlier today and I fold a hole compartment hidden off at the back of the cabin. It was loaded with rope and some electric lantern. Crazy how all of it was just sitting there untouched. As for the grub situation, all I could find on yesterday's hike were simple grapes and a few wild berries. Not sure how long stuff like that would be able to hold me over. I do think I'm good for now. Luna keeps telling me about if I see any wildlife, to stay away from it.

Honestly I don't disagree, but at this point it seems like that damn dog keeps following ME. I call it a dog because of its dog-like tendencies. I would be lying if I said It wasn't too adorable to ignore. It was laying at the edge of the doorway last night facing me. As much as I had not much interest, it's company made me feel better. I think I'll stick with the name Malos. It seems suitable. I haven't seen that bear I witnessed earlier again thankfully. I use that term very loosely, as that creature I had the misfortune of coming across that day was hardly that of one. I wonder if I actually even experienced it, my mind was still messed up after all. I honestly hope to not find out.

Day 3

Alright so today definitely was a good day. I guess you can call it good, or plain strange. After walking a long bit up and down the 20th parallel trail scavenging for anything edible practically, I made a quite unusual and definitely unexpected discovery. Sitting, plain as day next to the forest line about half a mile down the trail, was a fresh box of nuts and crackers. Like it had been just purchased out of the snack ile in the supermarket. This event alone had made me more confident in Luna's findings as well. However way these random items are making their way out here, it sure is convenient to my situation. The rope I found yesterday came in handy as well, the lower rocky sides of the ridge served as a perfect short cut from from the 20th parallel. Now I can easily access the secret lake near dead man's trench. I hope to continue on my knowledge and exploration of this area. From the info Luna has given me, I can only conclude that the this entire reserve is some sort of gated perimeter, or forbidden land. How she was able to figure out the parallels, is just beyond me still. Anyways, as I write this, I'm about to hammer in the other end of this rope to the cliff side. I really do put faith in my newfound and improving survival abilities.

Day 15

I will admit, it is hard to keep track of time out here. Something about it is so hypnotizing, like the passing of time becomes irrelevant after awhile. That's coming from Luna not me by the way. Although I can't say I disagree. So, I have a lot of catching up to do here I suppose. Over the past few days, I've began to feel more appreciative about my current state, and my future. The severe disconnect from the outside "real" world gets to everyone in a sense. It's not that I'm ambitious to leave, it's different. I feel unsafe. Even by the side of Malos at the doorway every night, things never really seem right. Like something very small, impractical, but yet very true in its existence is wrong. As well as that, the harsh realities of what is the cold night breeze constantly flowing through the still agape hole in the wall, keeping me from sleep. I still haven't got around to doing anything about it. Maybe it's just that good ol dog that keeps me from doing so. It's currently morning as I write this, just barely recovering from a somewhat devastating fall. I knew that old rope would give out eventually. About an hour ago I started down it on my normal morning routine scavenge for resources, about half way down it only took a slight crack sound to make me realize what was about to happen. Luckily the rope was fastened on the shorter end of the ridge. Halfway down was almost, maybe a 30 foot plunge down the rocks. One sprained arm later, here I am writing this. It sure is a damn good thing I'm a lefty. Also once again with no short way to the freshwater lake, so I'm gonna have to start burning the calories again. On the bright side of things, I do believe I'm getting closer to Luna as a friend. Or maybe just a rather considerable ally in this situation. We're both in this together, pretty much whether we like it or not. Somewhere miles away, there is someone else in the same state as me. Two of the most people lost people in the world, and yet I feel close. I might start writing in here more, as I've developed a habit of literally taking it everywhere I go.

Day 17

Last night I awoke to the sound of my wife's voice. She talked to me as if she were right next to me, like the good times I had only recently remembered. Her presence was the most soothing sensation I've felt in a long time, and for a moment, made me forget everything that had happened. It seemed so real to me, indescribably true. Only when I woke up this morning to Luna telling me about how she heard me in the middle of the night talking to someone, did it really hit me. That my emotions, and love for my wife, was still there. And it is here. Maybe my subconscious was trying to tell me some deep, meaningful statement. Either that, or my extremely dilapidated mind was refusing to put up with me after a 14 hour hike. Nevertheless, I am thankful for it. Recently I found another large carving ingrained in a nearby tree. This time, uncomfortably close by, and to my knowledge, may be a predatorial sign of some sort. This motivated me to finally patch up that doorway to the cabin. All it took was some leftover pieces of bark from a collapsed tree, and a little finesse. Not that that would stop anything bigger than me from entering if it truly desired. Regardless, the small entryway created by the gap of wood made a safe and easy way for me to get through, and maybe even Malos if he still had interest in me for some odd reason. Tomorrow I feel the need to get a better feel of the area, try my best to find another shortcut down the ridge.

Day 18
My plans to explore the surrounding area have been canceled by nature itself. The thunderstorm seemed to have spawned out of nowhere in the middle of the night, drenching the entryway. Yesterday night was also the last night I saw Malos at the door, diligently watching over me as usual. Clearly he had other plans rather than playing the roll of my soaked doormat this time. Each strike of lightning still sends shivers down my spine as I write this. The fear of loud, and abrupt noises are probably of rival to my only other fear of the unknown. At this point, it seems to have been going for days now. Hours pass as long as weeks as I stay up restless. I don't even bother guesstimating the time, and have no indication as of now that this storm will blow over any time soon. The worst part about this

predicament is the lack of communication I know have with Luna. Any time I tried to radio in, or call her always came back with a dead air signal, indicating that whatever line of contact we had before was being disrupted by the storm. I could understand why however, the power of this particular storm is constantly sending splashes of water bombarding the thin windows of the cabin. Along with winds that sound more or less like an unrealistic movie sound effect. In reality though, I can only hope this all lasts no more than the rest of the night, or I will officially be in a worse situation. Although I do consider myself lucky to some extent, the fact that this old place can withstand such force is incredible, and quite a fight it's putting up. I feel the foundations of the very floor beneath me radle and quake at every burst of thunder. Also, I wouldn't exactly consider it a good detail that I happen to lie at the highest point for literal miles. Either way, I'm still alive. The water pump refills itself on a regular basis, and has a process of collecting water that just so happens to fall from the sky as well. Food on the other hand, is the problem I may face if this doesn't let up soon. I will update again, once I'm able to successfully contact Luna, or at the very least overcome this storm. It may be awhile, it may not be.

Day 64

So, based off my last entry, I can safely conclude that it has infact been, awhile. Yes, that storm finally did blow over, and yes, I am addressing me or whoever long lost individual may be reading this in the future. And for the record, I don't exactly know how even at this point some crazy government agents haven't tracked my very position and taken me down. I keep circling countless amounts of scenarios in my head of what exactly could have gone down that humble day. The day that I, Reggie Green, managed to successfully escape not only the Denver county jail, but death row. Surely, I must be a national sensation, an international icon, written in textbooks to come. The fact is that I know where I am just as much as anyone else does I'm sure of it. Even now, a smile creeps across my face every time I imagine the expression of the warden when he came to escort a prisoner to the death chamber from an empty cell. It is one of the only priceless things that keep me entertained. Well, now that all that rambling is done, let's get to the point. It's day... what 60? I don't even know, I'm just making up numbers at this point. To cut to the chase, it's been a very long time. Not long enough for me to learn everything about this place that there is to know, and definitely not long enough to go completely insane. But I'm getting there. As a quick refresher, or a recap if you will: The storm that left off ravaging the area ended up making more problems than I first anticipated. I eventually passed out due to pure exhaustion and lack of energy the night of the last update. I woke up on the hard and very moist floor of the almost capsized cabin. The front window, overlooking the peak was cracked at the edges, along with a breach in my makeshift door. The radio, somehow ended up on the other end of the room in not so decent condition. When I finally gained my full awareness of the situation, I realized the biggest issue. A portion of the mountain had completely fallen off. Halfway across from the cabin and the cliff, became a huge pile of dirt, stone, and broken trees hundreds of feet below. Had it had been a little larger piece, no doubt the cabin would have gone with it. On the bright side of this, the slope the landslide had created made a smoother and safer shortcut down the ridge. The rest of the untouched rope I had left was just long enough to stretch to the bottom after I latched it to the side of a rock. I now had another, more full proof shortcut. Luna called me right after the storm and confessed on how she was sure I had died during the incident. She could easily see where the mountain had collapsed from her binoculars. She had also tried contacting me throughout the storm but as I mentioned, the signal was jammed beyond belief. Overall the new literal landslide did me well in my ventures back and forth from the hidden lake. Luna has been keeping me company, but not as much as she used to, and adding frequent mentions of uneasy feelings she's been experiencing. Strangely enough, in a general sense, I too have had them more often than before. They act as a cyclistic system, they come, usually leading to a slight anxiety episode, and go as quickly as they came. I can only accurately describe them as being similar to the feeling at the pit of my gut when I first came across dead man's trench so long ago. An eerie feeling of being hunted, studied, watched, entrapped, maybe all of the above. I still go there from time to time to gather resources, and each time I keep getting this damn sensation. Whatever it is, I would greatly appreciate it if it would simply leave me, Luna, maybe even that God forsaken dog that keeps following me alone. On a similar note, many more horrendous gashes have appeared on trees since the last time I wrote here. Three or more of them appearing overnight. Surprisingly, they seem to have deviated from their original pattern, and have began appearing further and further away from the 20th parallel. One of which I came across not even a week ago on a long hike off the grid in an effort to somewhat map my area. Two or so miles out, lie another large scratch. This one was far different from the rest I'd encountered. The entire tree that served host to the carving was completely toppled over. I'm talking about a good 20 foot tree, down in timbers from whatever caused it. I ruled out it simply being the aftermath of a lightning strike from the storm due to none of the surrounding area being affected. Nevertheless I still am skeptical. The sun also seems to be sinking quicker now than ever before. If my intuition is correct, and we are heading into a merciless winter, I surely will not make it through. Definitely not in my current vulnerable state. Yeah I know I'm not always a positive thinker but I think it's healthy to look at the negative side of things once in awhile. This way, you're less likely to be disappointed. Luna's trying to contact me right now, should probably see what's going on. See you soon.

Day 70

I have officially concluded that it is around day 70-ish, thanks of course to the help of my more time managed radio friend. The trees and now browning grass, along with the stern drop of temperature indicates my suspensions of a nearby winter were not far off. The glades of grass surrounding the cabin have become overwhelmingly tall, creating an almost not translucent camouflage with the pine trees. Something about it makes me feel more secure. Amazingly, Malos I guess decided he enjoys it too. Yesterday walking back from my water pump to see the wolf leisurely resting near the glades was the first time I'd seen him in weeks. I figured he'd take the winter off and do what any normal creature of his species does, but still no. I still force myself to talk to him on and off whenever the radio goes blank or I'm just straight up lonely. Which is almost a constant feeling now, only suppressed by the ever increasing eerie sensation, that occasionally morphs into a pure sense of dread. Spontaneous and unnatural dread. I assumed it to be the leading reason why I have yet to hear anything from Luna within the passed few days. The radio is silent on the other end. I'm still trying to figure out how I'm in someway experiencing the same thing as her almost on cue. Sometimes I still wonder the legitimacy of it all. As of now, the dread is coming back. I feel it beginning to devour me, as I do each time it hits out of nowhere. As much as I'd like to keep dwelling on this, I must continue preparing for the exponentially dropping temperatures. The sky itself has transformed from its original crisp blue status quo, to a more hazy dense orange. Complemented by the rather similar in shade ocean of trees. My worries for Luna become greater every second I go without her voice. I need her now more than ever. I need a break from all this.

"You know, I've been thinking about that idea you've had for a while now. If we meet up, we can share our resources." Luna's familiar voice echoed across the cabin room. I had once again passed out on the hardwood table, exhausted as ever. I thought it was rather funny how out of the many days that had passed since I last heard anything from her, she'd picked the most inconvenient time to finally break the silence. "

It just doesn't feel safe out here anymore. I think I need to move grounds." She added.

"You're right." I responded with a lackadaisical tone.

It was most likely only a few hours past sunset, and I had completely lost all energy from my anxiety. "

What do you think all this is?" I asked.

"Honestly, I haven't really been completely transparent about it but, ever since you got here, and I heard a random guy speaking to me for the first time in... well, forever... weird shit's been going down. The forest has been carved up, I still find whiskey bottles in the middle of a stream, and now it's come to me feeling physically in danger."

At this, I could only force myself to feel a deep feeling of guilt, like whatever the outlandish things happening to me, have now been propelled onto Luna. Through my windows, In the dim onset of moonlight, I could vaguely make out her campfire burning so far out over the reserve.

"Look Luna, I'm sorry, about all of this." I said still doozie.

"No, I'm the one who should be able to handle this better. I honestly should have just listened to you when you first told me about what you found at the trench. Instead, I've just been behind this radio being to myself." She replied.

"This is definitely not your fault Luna, I need to get things figured out and find a way out of here for the both of us."

As I said this, I noticed the slight speckle of light fade away, and a plume of smoke rising from the horizon. She was clearly getting ready to go somewhere.

"Are you okay?" I asked.

"I need to get out of here Reg. Don't worry, I got another place out a little further I'm gonna stay for now. Please, get some rest for yourself." The radio cut out.

Dead air.

Once the insomnia began to kick in however, I guessed I wasn't getting much sleep for awhile. I was right. I tossed and turned constantly that entire night on the uncomfortably hard cot bed. Every time I would feel myself slowly drifting off, my body jerked me back to life in a surge of anxiety. I could almost feel every fiber of my being becoming choked up. The very thought of sleep was painful, but my tired body was too out of it for anything near physical activity. After what seemed like hours of this, I finally managed to drift into the peaceful emptiness of sleep.

...

8. AMBUSH

It wasn't until I felt the blisteringly hot rays of sunlight hitting me when I awoke. I was facing the window giving my already swollen eyes a dosage of bright light as I opened them. It took awhile for them to adjust to my surroundings, but when they finally came around to it, what I saw shocked me beyond what I was prepared for. The front and main window of the cabin had been completely smashed in, destroyed, glass shattered everywhere. Some small shards even lay directly next to where I'd just been. The rest of the cabin seemed to the most bizarre effect, untouched.

Everything about it seemed so incredibly unnatural that at first, I could only use my sensible mind to dismiss it as strong winds. Until one detail completely debunked all of it. The radio I had placed on the wooden table next to me the night before, was gone. Taken clean off the thing, not a scratch or alteration to the position of the table. I checked frantically around the room searching under and on all the objects in the cabin, which wasn't much. Everything had been exactly the way I remembered seeing them last. Even the crappy makeshift wooden door I had constructed, untouched.

Nothing but a smashed window, and now the absence of my only means of communication. I wondered to myself how in the hell I could have slept through all of the obvious commotion. At this point, I knew there was no actual way that I was alone out here. Someone was playing with me, possibly Luna as well. No animal could possibly break through a window, steal a walkie-talkie, and leave like nothing had happened. I knew that as a certainty.

I realized my suspicions were confirmed when I noticed the freshly made tracks leading to, and away the cabin window. Despite my lack of knowledge for animal tracks in general, I could still safely identify the different looks of a human shoe and anything else. It was an unusually hot day, more so than it had been for months with the oncoming winter air. It was clear enough to where I no longer needed binoculars to see the smoldering plume of smoke rising in the distance.

Luna couldn't have gotten that far overnight. And if she did make it to this so-called, other place, then maybe she'd already try to contact me and realize someone else had my radio. If not, I'd have to come the wilderness all day until I found it. I viewed the radio as a more important asset than anything else I could gather out there. Before I could ensue on my trip, I noticed a particular sound echoing from the distance at the brim of my hearing abilities.

The feature of the sound that grabbed my attention more than anything else was the familiarity to it. I knew I had heard the sound sometime before, but I just could not bring myself to fully remember. It manifested itself as a very slight high pitched buzzing emanating from deep within the wilderness. Sounding similar to the sirens I heard in my dreams before all of this started. I began downslope of the ridge where many large piles of rocks and debris still lie from the avalanche. Even though I had many days, and multiple falls to get the hang of making it all the way down the huge hill without messing up, I still struggled to adjust to it. Knowing my intention to retrieve back my only significant way to communicate is what drove me to put particularly more effort into this hike.

Along with the anticipation to possibly show the perpetrator a piece of my feelings towards the matter. Thinking about this though, gave me a bad feeling at the pit of my being. I came to a realization that I was delving into the complete uncharted woods with no means of self defense, protection, or preservation. I was barehanded with nothing more than my very slight knowledge of the geography in between the 20th and 80th parallels.

Whether or not there was a high chance of even encountering the person who did this, I knew for a fact that the wilderness around me was inherently dangerous. An I might as well have just slid down the ridge with nothing but a "come get me" sign on for how unprepared I was. I however, with what had just happened, I had nothing to lose. I continued on through the forest on an off grid trail I discovered during my exhibitions. I called this particular path the enchanted trail, as it served as a shortcut towards the hidden lake. The trees on either side of the trail seemed to curve inward and formed a tunnel appearance.

I trusted my hearing to guide me closer to the source of the now diminishing buzzing sound, which also grew greater down the path. After only a good 10 minutes of hiking, I saw that the ground below me had transformed from a fine textured gravel, to moist mud. The entire area that now lay ahead of me could be classified as a mini-swamp, puddles of rainwater gathered from the storm soaking into the ground. I scanned the land ahead of me for a decent way across until I noticed, a deep and well defined trail of feet leading straight through the mud.

The clear and intentional tracks were almost too obvious to believe. Each step was separated by a massive gap, indicating the fast pace of whoever was here before me. There was someone out here, and for whatever reason why they got so close to me, I knew they would know my first response to the situation. To do exactly what I was doing at that moment. Instantly, a crushing feeling of realization swept over me. They were trying to lead me somewhere, possibly right to them. Completely empty handed.

There was simply no way any person all the way out here would be dumb enough to make their trail so clear. I was not about to risk myself to an ambush, or trap of some sort. My mind raced through ideas of what do do. At that moment, my general intention of wanting to escape this place once and for all left me, and my brain shifted into total survival mode. Instead of continuing forward, I did a 180 into the complete wilderness off the grid. My basic knowledge of the area gave me incite to the general place I was headed to.

Anywhere away from any kind of setup was my true destination. The pine trees turned into cottonwood as I made my way through the course terrain. Something about the enchanted forest made time seem to stand still, especially in such a frantic mood. I could have guessed hours had passed when I made it to the tall grass fields that bordered the hidden beach. The lake, and twin waterfalls were visible to me. The grass itself appeared to have doubled its height since the last time I paid the place a visit.

The storm must have been responsible for the complete resurrection of plant life, the area looked like an oasis of green and lush to the surrounding brown autumn. The lake, with its vibrant blue, emphasized the contrast. When I reached the beach, the sound had almost completely disappeared, and morphed into an unrecognizable ringing, like the sound of switching broadcast channels on the radio.

It was very faint, but plainly noticeable. The trees that bordered the beach, and wooded area around the secret lake were completely scratched and had their bark torn away. Half of them looked like nothing more than petrified logs protruding out of the ground. Anxiously, I continued my search for the source of the entrancing noise. The closer that I felt I got to the epicenter of it, the further away it became. I traveled down the beach closer to the dead man's trench, chasing after the phantom sound.

As I came across the opening to the tree line, creating a natural path near the trench, the sound completely stopped. I was now surrounded in what I could only consider to be complete silence. No animal, gust of wind, or even the rushing waters of the lake made a peep. Standing at the border between the trees, and the beach, I felt my gut tell me to look into the further into the forest. A feeling that I thought was sheer intuition, but also felt like something was calling out to me.

As I did, the very first thing my eyes came to rest at was the large wooden sign I had witnessed ages ago. The wooden plank that served somewhat as an ancient testament to the experiences of whomever may have been there last. It was still perched up against the same tree, which didn't even seem to have changed since I last saw it months ago.

Something about the sign however, seemed off. Everything about my surroundings were to a great extent similar to what they've always been, the sign though, wasn't. It's very position, and esthetic, seemed completely wrong. I walked up to it, barely being illuminated under the massive tree. Kneeling down to get a better look at it made me even more perplexed. The writing I recalled seeing before, signed by "Austin 1803" was more vibrant and legible. It no longer seemed ancient, it looked newly replaced or refurbished. Before dismissing it as my own heavily impressionable imagination, I realized that the sign was elevated a bit off the ground to the slightest amount.

I gasped as I slipped my fingers under, and into a large open space. I felt a stream of cool air coming from the space. With one exasperated and forceful pull, I yanked the rather heavy sign off its hinges. I now knew it wasn't a sign, it was a hatch. Instantly a gust of chilled air met my face as I stared down into the hole. I was expecting to see darkness, but I saw a very faint light coming from the bottom of a wooden ladder leading down to it.

I couldn't bring myself to fully believe what I was witnessing. My mind began to race at whether I should enter the decrepit shaft or not. I started to think of Luna, and were she could've been at that moment. If she was even safe. After I debated with myself I decided the fight for answers was worth the endeavor down the shaft.

Taking the first step made me want to reconsider the entire idea. Chills ran up my spine as a very deep anxiety once again poured over me. After the amount of time I'd spent here, I knew that this particular feeling of anxiety only spelt bad things. I fought off my hesitation and continued downwards. The shaft was long, but carefully illuminated enough so I could barely make out the dirt walls. I reached the last step of the ladder when my foot hit the hard concrete floor with a thud. I wasn't expecting the sudden landing, and fell back off the ladder into a large room. It was impeccably huge and extended further down the underground chamber.

All of the walls were lined with computers, and monitors. Each one was set up in three different stations aligned next to each other. I would be lying if I said I didn't almost shit myself when I saw what was on each monitor. Every single one had an individual camera feed on it, recording everything in the area from many angles. There was even a camera placed somewhere near the entry of the shaft I had just been. Dozens of different monitors, each intruding on everything around, even my cabin way back at the ridge was filmed from someplace I had never noticed. I was being watched, all this time, probably Luna as well.

The sight of it all made me sick to my stomach. Everything was being monitored. Angered, and confused, I made my way over to one of the desks in front of an array of nine of them. I instantly noticed the crate next to the desk. Inside it, sure enough, was my long lost radio. I grabbed and inspected it, expecting to see it broken or tampered with. Yet, it was in the same condition as I'd remembered. There were loose papers left in the crate, some of which had writing. I was hoping to find some answers to why this was all taking place when I examined them.

Ironically, they left me with more questions and concerns that I'd had ever before. Each piece of notebook paper had written dialogue on each page, noting everything I'd said to Luna, and all the places I'd been to in the last two months. Each inscription had time and dates to every slightest thing I did.

"*7:10 pm leaves cabin.*"

One line below; "*8:45 pm returns to cabin. Carrying wood. Steak out tmr at 3.*"

"*2:20 pm 9-12 boss doesn't want knowledge of the gate slipping out from the female. Signal jammed.*"

At this I realized that whoever these creeps were, they were definitely spying on me, and writing down all of the information I had gotten out of Luna as well.

"*Luna Robinson age: 30-40? Survival skill: decent. Steak out at 5 tmr DON'T GET TOO CLOSE*"

The notes finished on that page. It only took one paragraph of the next page to make me too angry to continue on. It seemed to be an inscription of a conversation between two other people.

"*Honestly though, don't bother with the female. He's our guy.*"

"You think they suspect anything yet?"

"She knows, it's only a matter of time until either she speaks, or he finds us. But that's what the boss wants."

"They're both scared."

I crumpled the paper and hurled it across the massive room in shear rage. All of what I had read drowned out my anxiety and fueled my fury over the fact that Luna and I were being gamed, and studied. Like lab rats. I scanned through the rest of the papers only seeing more countless amounts of these recorded conversations.

Every small detail that I had ever given out over the radio was documented. I thought of contacting Luna in that moment until my more logical side took over me. Maybe that's what they wanted me to do. Now that I knew they heard every single peep out of me through this blasted thing, and were more than capable of jamming the signal, I thought twice. Out of the many things I had kept myself from telling her over time, I knew this was to big to be one of them. I was not to any extent careful to remain obscure. I made my presence quite apparent in the destruction of their "notes". When I made my way back to the top, I finally convinced myself to confess my findings to Luna, and also subsequently letting those people be aware as well. Either way, I had little choice in matter. Luna, didn't take it lightly.

9. ANSWERS

"You found what!?" She asked loudly after I explained everything I saw. I had the courage to tell her about the personal notes written about us.

"There's an underground layer full of computers, cameras, and they're using it to observe us." I responded. "They have literal pages of notes and documents written about us, and a crazy amount of personal data about me and you." I continued.

"Well what the hell is this all about? Where even are you?" She asked frantically.

"Down by the lake, I don't know how I even came across it but it was just there. Someone took the radio from my cabin, and just left it here."

"Reggie, this isn't making any sense... I just... how?" Luna's voice began to morph into a paranoid scramble of words.

"I don't know." I replied firmly, making my way back up the trail I came from.

A few moments passed before she spoke again.

"So you're saying not only is someone else out here, but they broke into the cabin, took your radio and is monitoring us both with extremely high tech equipment." She summarized.

"Yeah, I don't get any of it either." I exclaimed.

The walk through the mystical forest of cottonwood trees made me relax more than I thought was natural. I had just been through a situation that could indicate a potential threat to both me, and my radio companion that I've spent so long getting to know and understand. Now only to find out all of it was being baited out of me by some creep that's been out here with us the whole time. I struggled to wrap my mind around the whole of the situation. All I could concentrate on in that given moment, was the absence of that exhausting feeling of dread that I had lingering over me for the longest time.

It was for once, completely gone. I felt dignified, and in control of myself for once. My questions for what exactly I read in those entries however, were not yet fully answered. They left me with copious amounts of questions to everything I thought was real in my experiences in this wilderness. I subliminally felt like a puppet being mindlessly controlled by some far off master, effortlessly pulling the strings. I also couldn't help thinking of how I could have fallen directly into a intricately formulated setup. Had this all been some bait?

One last question pumped into my mind that I just knew I had to get an answer for.

"Hey are you there?" I asked the radio.

"I'm not going anywhere around here anymore Reg." She replied.

"Hey uh, I wanted to ask... One of the papers that I skimmed through said something about you actually knowing about some of this... what, does that mean?"

"Uh... I'm not sure."

"Luna, it said something about you knowing. What does that mean!?" I demanded.

"Okay I've known about the weird shit out here for a while Reggie. Alright? I've been out here for a long time and you know this. I never told you because you were already confused and I wasn't about to make it worse." She confessed.

"Wait, so you've known that there is someone else out here the whole time?" I asked.

"I can guarantee the only other sad, lost person who I ever knew to be out here was you. And now that I know differently, I'm not sure anything else even matters." She said.

"So, what now?" I asked.

"You've asked me that so many times now Reg." She said in a slight chuckle. "But this time, I don't have an answer for you."

I broke out of the cottonwood forest into a clearing as she said this. I could see the trailhead that lead to the 20th parallel in the distance. The sun, slowly submerging itself into the horizon casted a bright orange across the sky in a vibrance like nothing I'd seen before.

"I can guarantee one more thing. These woods, they aren't what you think they are." Luna said. "I know you've been doing this for a while now, and probably think you know the basics of how things work out here, but you don't." She added.

Every minute of that day that went by I felt myself realize how much I didn't actually know Luna. The only other voice that I've ever heard in that new reality of my life.

"What is that supposed to mean?" I asked almost weirded out.

"Just stay safe out there Reggie. Honestly. I'm going to try to find a way out of all this." She replied.

I still trusted her, no doubt about it. I didn't have any plans to suspend my trust with Luna especially now that I knew we were practically being hunted. However I simply could not stop relaying the documents I had uncovered in my head. It didn't make any sense how whoever was doing this could know so much about me with such little time. I remembered the personal data entries that displayed info about me that I didn't share with anyone. And I'm sure goes the same with Luna.

Along with all of the technology, most of which was so advanced I'd never even seen before. I could have very well been watched all the way up to this point. It made me feel more like none of what I was witnessing was even remotely real.

The trees began to cast vast shadows on the dusty ground below me. The very last bit of daylight fought to escape from the horizon. In that moment, I remembered the wolf that I had become accustomed to. Good ol Malos. I had not been around his cheerful presence in a while. Even it's appearance at my doorstep every night gave me a sense of comfort. Regardless of me not doing my due diligence on his behavior, I still expected to see him from time to time. But I hadn't.

Maybe he was still out there somewhere. Maybe he was still with me just, following at a distance to keep my behind safe. Or maybe he left me, to do what I could only guess an actual wild animal should do. Something about him reminded me of my wife. Everything she did that stuck out in my mind as beautiful was somehow being reflected off that wolf, which is why I treasured its company. The company I did not treasure on the other hand, was the very slight amount of light given off by the moon while on foot.

One thing Luna for some reason felt the need to emphasize more than I thought was necessary, would be the bad habit of being out at night. Her words echoed through me like a mega phone. "You wake up in the morning, the wilderness wakes up at night." She would always say to me. I had somehow managed to be out all day simply looking for straight forward answers, but still came back with nothing. Without wasting anymore of the already draining daylight, I continued onward up the path to what I got used to calling home. It was my home.

...

Only minutes later did it become absolutely pitch black. The chilled air of the winter front seemed to use its full force against me. I was completely empty handed besides the radio that I had most rightfully retrieved in my efforts. I had no light, water, food, or navigation. My bareboned self suffered the consequences due to my lack of preparation of this whole ordeal. The trail I continued on only seemed to become windier, and more unstable in areas.

My eyes were forced to adjust to the complete absence of all light anywhere, aside from the very faint almost undetectable light from the stars above me, and mostly eclipsed moon. I had recently forgotten the harsh hike required to take "the long way" back to the parallel after the fortunate landslide event. It only took a little bit of time for me to spoil myself.

I began to reflect on all of the things I went throughout in this reserve. All of the hardships, struggles, and perseverance I had managed to pull off. All in an attempt at seeing the big picture. I always thought, just maybe it would help shed some light on the whole thing. I also recognized that it never did.

Before I could delve deeper into the rabbit hole which was my own mind, I stopped in my tracks. In the very back of my mind, I could make out a very slight sound escaping from the tree line. I truly wanted to believe it was my imagination especially after the events that transpired, but I couldn't. I continued forward and pretended to not pay any attention to it. The forest around me became dead silent as it had before at random intervals. Every step that I took made a loud, and prevalent impression in my environment.

The feeling of accomplishment that I had achieved today, was quickly drowned out by a familiar deep pitched feeling of fear. By my own memory, I could promptly conclude that I wasn't far from the cabin at that point, after all, I had been making my way up the path for ages. Each step forward that I proceeded to take seemed to create a bigger disturbance in the ambiance of the forest. I felt the crunching of dirt beneath my worn down shoes echo off the trees around me.

The echo in itself came off as odd to me however. This certain echo that I was hearing didn't match up to my surroundings to any extent. With common sense, one can conclude that an echo is a result of sound bouncing off walls and mountains to form the infamous repetitive noise. The problem with all of that was, there were no mountains around anywhere. The area for the most part, was completely flat. I had only been traveling on a slight uphill curve the entire way.

Nevertheless, each step I took formed an almost identical mimic of itself afterward. Confused and annoyed at this, I once again stopped dead in my tracks. Nothing. Everything around me was silent to the degree that I couldn't believe, as if the world had stopped spinning. I checked my surroundings, and pinched myself to help maintain my sanity just in case. Up ahead of me was a curve in the path that led uphill.

I now knew I couldn't have been more than a few hundred yards away from my safe haven and refuge. Nervously, I continued on at a considerably slower pace than before so I could carefully analyze the echo. It seemed louder now, approaching me from all directions yet, I still could not determine how it could be occurring. As I turned the tight and jagged corner, I began to formulate an idea. It was a far out and outlandish thought that flowed through me, but I knew I had to try it. I took more steps, one after another in a very organized pattern. My heart now racing at intense speeds, I went through with my plan.

The very next step I took, I stopped barely giving space between the ground and my foot. Crunch. The sound came from behind me. It in itself practically put my already exhausted heart out of its misery. Without any hesitation, I booked it forward up the path faster than I thought was even physically possible. Behind me, I heard the footsteps closing in on me, just as frantically as mine were. I dared not look back at whoever or whatever was now full on chasing me through the dark wilderness. Something in me knew that it had to have been someone involved in the theft of my radio. I didn't want to speculate, the only goal in that given moment was to make it back up to the cabin at the 20th parallel that was now clearly visible over the ridge. I sprinted faster uphill, ignoring all of the ways my body was telling me to stop as I began to feel my life pass before me. The frantic sprinting behind me morphed into a distant pitter patter, but I didn't care. I juked every tree that was rooted on top of the ridge and burst through the barricade of wood at the door of the cabin.

....

10. ICOLATED

I awoke the following morning lying face down on the hard floor of the cabin. Wood splinters and pieces had flown everywhere after I burst through my makeshift door. The biggest mass of it, rested across the entire room, next to the radio that had also presumably flown across the cabin. Disoriented and drowsy, I managed to pick myself up and hobble across the room to retrieve the radio.

Glass had still remained from the recent break in that occurred which formed a rather uncomfortable combination with small pieces of broken wood and bark. The place was a complete mess. From what it had been from my first encounter, I could only feel bad for whoever had invested the time to arrange all of it. Not that it made any sense to me. The radio, which I picked up half under a chunk of wood debris seemed to be on its last legs in terms of condition. Half of the antenna was broken off only after what I assumed happened the night before.

My memory was foggy in the moment, but I most definitely could make out the fact that I no longer viewed this place as safe, let alone pleasant. What Luna had said in its entirety was completely accurate. Everything about my situation was beginning to seem way off from what I first thought it was. I began to wipe off the dust and grime from the weathered radio. With the condition it was in, I was having my doubts of if I would ever be able to use it again, and from what I could understand, I'm sure that they wanted it like that. Whoever *they* were.

Regardless of anything else, there was no arguing against the fact of other people being out there, and clearly without the best intentions. After profusely cleaning and managing the radio to the best of my ability, I wiped off some of the dirt that accumulated on my own face. The only option I had ever been given in terms of sanitation was the water pump out the back of the cabin. It didn't really offer much of an opportunity to always stay ahead of my hygiene, so dirt on my face wasn't an unusual occurrence. However, I noticed only after stroking my face that fresh blood was still leaking out of a wide gash on my cheek. I realized that in the flight or fight decision that I was prompted to make the night before, my apparent flight action, came with some repercussions. Most of the blood had already formed a natural scab, so the bleeding wasn't much of an issue.

My only concern was to contact Luna as soon as I could to try to figure out an ultimate way out of here. This time, I knew to be more careful, considering the obvious fact that my location was easily tracked through the radio. I tried the communicate button on it. At first, nothing, followed by a mild static sound after a few seconds. I could tell that it was heavily damaged. I held down the button for as long as I could to try to maintain a decent signal. Two or three minutes passed of this before I started to vaguely make out a voice under the static. It was Luna's voice.

The interference was still too high to even remotely understand what she was saying.

"Hello? Luna, can you hear me?" I yelled into it hoping to get a somewhat legible response. Still, nothing but a gobbled up cluster of words covered by static.

I fiddled with the mangled antenna hoping to make some kind of difference. I heard the fairly panicked tone of Luna through the white noise. There was no doubt that she had been trying to contact me for a while. I rushed out of the cabin and roamed around the grassy top of the ridge to find any type of location where the signal wouldn't be jammed. I shuffled over to the edge of the rock slide and gazed over the vast expanse of nothingness. Something I had for sure became accustomed to at that point. I felt my cheeks begin to contort in the weirdest way, forming a sensation I had not felt in ages.

I felt myself failing to hold in the tears as they streaked down my scared face. I couldn't even remember the last time I had cried before then, emotion and feeling itself seemed to be absent from me since it all started. So much of it was finally making its escape. My face was quickly dried by the dry breeze flowing through the orange sky. For the first time, I had actually felt hopeless, and at a complete loss. My entire world had caved in similar to the rocks and mountainside below me.

Half of my old rope, still protruding out of the gravel. The static grew dimmer as I continued to stare into the horizon.

"Should I give up?" I asked myself.

At that moment, my mind truly felt like doing so. However, my conscience knew I couldn't. As the last remaining drop of pure emotion fell from my eye, I turned to see the lone tree standing firm on the cliff side. Wiping my eyes to have a better idea of what I was looking at, I confirmed what I saw. The mangled and scratched bark stretching from top to bottom of the thing.

It had now reached me.

Looking over the seas of trees below me, each one was now host to those horrific scratches. They had been slowing spreading, and now, right next to my cabin, couldn't have been etched any earlier than overnight. I dropped the radio in that moment of pure fear.

"What the hell does this mean?" I yelled out loud as I began power walking towards the tree.

When I got over to it, I noticed the rest of the forest below the cliff. Every direction was the same damn thing. The spring months should have surely started the regrowth process by now, yet everything looked dead beyond recognition. All sharing the signature scrape down each trunk.

"WHAT DOES THIS MEAN!?" I yelled even louder this time.

The only answer I received in return was the hushed voice of the forest breeze echoing around me.

I was now one man, standing at the edge of the 20th parallel, and the edge of reality itself. Nothing made sense anymore. I picked up the radio from where I had left it. Now, completely silent, I made my way with it back into the cabin.

Sitting on the still in good condition chair, I placed the radio on the desk in front of me. Just, started at it, incompetently. As if I was waiting for it to fulfill all of my needs. The broken window made the wind a clear passage straight to my face.

It felt good to just let go of it all for a while, to forget it all existed, and simply enjoy the fresh air.

Nothing seemed to matter anymore, especially to me. Luna, I didn't know what mattered to her, but the deep part of me knew she cared for me as much as I did for her. Even though we were now separated by static, and miles of uncharted wilderness, I felt the connection never loosen.

I also noticed that everything in the cabin had once again been restored to an almost perfect state. Refurbished, and cleaned entirely. Only allowing the smashed window as a mild discrepancy. I couldn't help but simply smile at the sight of it.

I gazed back down towards the radio. I had known what I needed to do for awhile, only then did I want to tell Luna. Not caring who would hear, if even anyone, I spoke into it.

"I'm gonna find a way out. I will make it out. We're both gonna make it."

No response.

Without hesitation, I started rummaging through the supplies I had gathered under the desk. I used a piece of burlap I had found lying on the path side, and created a form of a makeshift bag, decent enough to hold a variety of items. Some of the random untouched foodstuffs carelessly left around the area that I had picked up over time did do some good for the arrangement. Luckily I had a good memorization of the locations of streams in the general area, where I could hydrate.

The majority of streams I had known were victim to the harsh conditions of nature, leaving behind only a riverbed, or ravine of rocks. Most of which stretched down to dead man's trench. I used them to guide my way into the uncharted territory with the absence of Luna's intuition.

By the time I knew I was miles away from any trailhead, path, or landmark I could identify, the trees around me, along with nature itself began to take back its normal shape. Not a single piece of bark with a large scrape was to be seen anywhere. The sound of ambient crows and other wildlife began to fill the late-winter tree branches. For the vastness of my journey, the sights ahead of me never seemed to change. The grass got greener the further I traveled, revealing the true extent of how wrong the area of the 20th parallel was. How mained and dead it was compared to anywhere else.

I had no means of knowing, but my intuition had a firm sense of being able to identify my direction. The sun of course, rose in away from my cabin and set beyond it. The sky was my only trustable compass. I followed it throughout the day, and dropped more useless items I had been carrying with me that were slowing me down. Further I traveled through the now orange toned Colorado wilderness and coming across fewer sources of water, which concerned me regardless of how well energized I was.

Now hours into the hike, an opening in the woods made itself clear to me. This one was large, bigger in radius than any ordinary forest clearing. On both sides, the tree line seemed to break off into separate directions, creating a long streak of open area. A very large, and emasculated boulder, which seemed to have been eroding away for eons lay in the center. It was tall enough to make surrounding trees pale in their height.

Something about it, however, felt altered. There seemed to be a clear stairway carved into it leading to the top. I climbed it. There was a small flat surface at the top, which I assumed was used as a lookout point. Far off in the direction I'd come from, with a mild squint, I saw none other than the 20th parallel ridge, with my cabin being a small dot sitting atop of it. I had really come that far. There was no doubt in my mind that I was close to Luna, I had to have been.

The once light breeze had now morphed into a rather violent wind, dropping the temperature a considerable amount. I switched my line of sight to the west to analyze how long I had left before sundown. The bright orange face of the sun was making itself clear in the sky yet was barely brushing above the coarse treetops of the forest.

Time was most definitely limited. I struggled down the rough face of the dilapidated rock, practically stumbling to my feet back on the surface. Placing one firm hand on my side, I rhetorically felt the radio for any vibrations or whispers. Of course, none. I kept playing scenarios in my mind on how exactly I would react if that were to change. If I were to hear the shrill voice of Luna, or even anyone else through that radio once again. The thought was intimidating to me. I had known that the only reasonable explanation for the loss of all communication with my trusted long range partner was none other than the signal being blocked. "The other people", as I referred to them, had to have knowingly done so in an effort to slow me down from figuring all of this out once and for all. I wasn't giving them the satisfaction this time however, I had everything planned out. There was no way I was about to mindlessly fall into another trap.

Noticing the dirt on the now tattered remains of clothes I wore, I brushed myself off and carried on into the continuum expanse of trees. The sun, now almost completely masqueraded by the thick canopy above me, left a near pitch black area devoid of anything other than rows of countless trunks. All of them, seemingly completely untouched by the winter conditions that had just passed, created a whole separate world of the lush landscape beneath the protection of treetops.

I continued onward through it, passing more of the endless untainted bark which I had missed seeing.

Ages passed as I caught myself constantly checking the radio for any sign of life, only to be let down again. The pack of useful materials I had brought with me began to strain me as I continued lugging it along. Out of all the cheerio boxes I had brought, only one of them was down to the last handful.

My mind was focused so purely on the mission, I'm sure for the most part, it had forgotten what food even was. Most likely my sense of time along with that.

Through what honestly felt like hours I savaged the dark lush underwoods for any sign of life anywhere. The entire time, never seeming to get darker despite the slivers of late sunset light that slipped through the canopy at times. Before I could come to a full train of thought, I found myself sat up against one of the massive tree trunks, out of breath and exhausted.

I felt my feet throbbing with the feeling of extreme mileage setting in. I rested my head back and sighed in utter relief. I sat there for a good 10 minutes simply examining my life decisions and questioning my own reasoning.

"Was this even worth it?" I said to myself. "Now that I think about it, I think I've fully retained my memory." The forest's silent acknowledgment to the statement motivated me to recap. I remembered everything about why I was here to begin with. The man in the red suit, the court hearing, the cell, the pipe, and that damn radio. Everything was completely clear to me at that point. And somehow, I knew that that red suited man must have had a part in formulating all of this. There was nothing in me that wanted to reject that theory. From the very moment I met him, the last face I now had no problem whatsoever remember him making towards me. All of it was beginning to add up.

A distant difference in the normal sound pattern distracted me. The clear sound of running water. The direction it was coming from was a far more open and brighter section of the canopy, giving way to a small distant creek. Something I wouldn't have paid much mind to hadn't I remembered Luna's own description of her camp.

With that, I fought myself to once more pick up my own weight. Even if it was only one last time.

Once back on my feet, I made it over to the rushing stream, which was further away, and quite a fair bit larger than it appeared. Everything about it matched exactly to what Luna had said. The birch tree trunks seemed to follow the steam down forever into the distance. Noticing that it was only a few inches deep, I had no problem crossing over onto what was clearly a man made trail.

Part of it hugged the edge of the stream, to where I was, it broke off and continued on. I slightly smiled as a whiskey bottle off in one of the bushes caught my eye. I knew I had made it.

11. LUNA

I traveled further up the hardly visible path towards what looked like a small wooden sign protruding from the brush. The sign itself was very dimly transcribed, seeming hundreds of years old at the sight of it. On it, simply stated:

"80th Parallel".

Half of the wood supporting it was broken off and mended into the soil, allowing it to stick out like a sore thumb even in the worst lighting conditions.

"Luna!?" I called out into the air hoping for some kind of answer. "It's Reg!" I added.

A few stray crows cawed in return to my desperate attempt. Only a few meters from the sign a nearby camp was visible, with a still smoldering plume of smoke which I could begin to smell at a distance. To my surprise, there was an entire other cabin sitting in the corner of the clearing, striking in similarity to the 20th parallel.

Stray cloths and cardboard boxes lay around the area of the now almost extinguished fire. Most of which seemed relatively freshly placed. As if the area had been abandoned in a rush. More things caught my attention, such as a hand drawn map of what appeared to be an entire area of the forest placed leisurely next to a foldable chair. Including parts that I wasn't even aware of.

A position was marked right where I had pictured my cabin to be as: "Reggie" along with a poorly drawn stick figure with a beard. If anything, that was the first time I had seen a depiction of myself since my mug shot back at the prison. Clearly, she'd been observing me more than I thought. Many other places had been marked near dead man's trench, one which I thought was interesting. "Those spying pricks" was marked near the location of the underground base practically right next to the trench.

Folding up the map, I placed it in my pack as a reference to where I was headed. The sun almost touching the horizon now, I knew that time was one of the most valuable assets that I had left, and now was the most scarce. The cabin placed cozily in the tree line was remarkably similar to mine. Everything up to the same water pump on the side. The sun was setting behind it, which made it impossible to have any idea of what was going on inside. I made my way up the ramp to it and hesitated at the door. I reached down towards my side again and felt the outline of the radio still strapped to me. Taking one deep breath, I went in.

...

Inside was brighter than the outside. It was very clear that she had been living in the thing far longer than I'd been here. I was amazed to see an entire radio setup sitting on the desk next to an entire bookshelf. Around the walls were presumably pages of research books ripped out and taped. And of course, no Luna. I hadn't seen any handheld radio in sight so I imagined that she had packed at least that. Still baffled at everything in front of me, I continued towards the desk and the radio equipment. It was mostly a simple microphone and a receptor box. Next to it, were binoculars placed on top of some loose papers and another crudely drawn impression of me.

A journal was placed next to a clutter of old looking books on the next table over. I was about to flip over the first page before I stopped myself.

"This is a friend's personal experience. Just leave it like that." I thought to myself.

I trusted Luna, and I had definitely come to know who she was as a person. I guess that's simply what happens when two people are separated by miles of nothingness with two radios and a whole lot of time. When I turned to leave the cabin, I stopped at the gaze of something I hadn't seen for ages.

Myself.

Sitting on a box across the cabin was a large wooden mirror. In it, was a very lost looking person, along with a now unkempt beard I had practically forgotten was there. I rubbed my hand down my cheek and felt the whiskers that I had become accustomed to for so long. The thought that I had come from cleanly shaven for my humble trip to the electric chair, to here was unyieldingly amazing.

My hair also seemed to have lightened from all the sun my body wasn't use to being confined in that cell. I was officially a wild man. A true freak of nature. The only thing separating me from other animals was my pack and my radio. Seeing the light slowly deplete from the camp out the window, making the dim fire more noticeable was my key to keep moving. I knew my trek to escape was nowhere near complete.

Walking out the door into a wall of pure campfire sent was refreshing to me. Some bright stars were beginning to leak through now, awaiting their signal from the moon to show themselves completely. I pulled out the map from the pack and looked closer towards the edge of it. Only a few inches from the 80th parallel marked "Camp" on the map, was a simple line and row of x's. There was no markings or details, the map simply stopped there.

I had, of course, no way of knowing if Luna had ever even traveled that far out, but it was convincing enough to me. I had to have been close. Without waiting, I left the map back where I found it and continued into the dark uncharted wilderness. The sun just barely delivering its last dose of red light into the sky. I was in no way in shape to continue on, but I forced myself to. For the both of us.

It couldn't have been more than an hour into the hike that I felt that familiar buzz near my waist. Without a seconds delay, I grabbed my radio and spoke into it.

"Hello!? Hello? Luna is that you?" I asked excitedly.

It took awhile for an answer, but this time there definitely was one.

"Hey Reggie, yeah it's me."

"Oh my god it's been absolutely forever, I can't believe I haven't been able to call you." I replied.

"Yeah, uh, I know. Um... you've probably left camp by now huh?"

"Yeah listen, about that, I never got a chance to tell you. I'm going to find a way outta here in no time. We both are getting out of here I promise." I assured her.

"Ha... huh, well, thanks, Reg but uh, I'm not sure if you can do that." She replied.

"Wa-what do you mean? I've packed up all my crap and I've made it all the way out here passed your place which you weren't at. Where even are you anyways? Aren't you okay!?" I rambled.

"Woah Woah, hold on there. Remember Reg, one question at a time. First off I am alright, and *you're* the one that I've been concerned about."

I started continuing on through the now completely pitch black woods. With only the full moon creeping through the treetops as my lamp.

"Yeah, I thought you'd make it out there so I left you that map. Hope you enjoyed my portrait of you." She added.

I smiled at this and replied. "I most certainly did. I left it there for you though for old times sake I guess."

She sighed. "Yeah, I honestly wish I could've been there. You-you're not still there... right?" She asked worryingly.

"No, why?"

"Reggie, I left for a reason, it's not safe there, or god knows anywhere anymore. That's what I mean. I think they're trying to push us out, and... I don't know. I don't think there is an 'out'".

I took a moment to process this information.

"What exactly happened Luna?" I asked seriously.

She took a while to respond. She finally did after what seemed like ages.

"I woke up last night to a figure at my window, just facing me. I couldn't see what they were doing, but I knew they were watching me. Before I even reacted, they just... walked off. Like nothing happened. I guess that was, kinda like the last straw for me, Reg."

I didn't know how to respond to this, all I could do was mutter a simple

"wow."

"Yeah..." she responded.

"Packed up shop and booked it. Now I'm kinda just out here. Alone. I figured being on the run might be a bit safer for now."

"Do you uh, have you ever been near that line you drew on the map?" I asked intently.

"That's the fence Reg, that is the edge of *this* place. And only once. There are no openings, not one exit, just... nothing. It's just that simple."

"You're not just gonna be there saying there's nothing we can do about this right Luna?" I said this as the signal began to fade. The pure white noise now once again filled my ears, then turned to dead air. I wasn't about to let this one fly, however.

I shook the radio sporadically in a fruitless attempt to get back Luna. Of course to no avail.

12. ESCAPE

I had been out for a long enough time that I hadn't even noticed the sheer level of darkness that surrounded me. My eyes had adjusted to it, but it was really hitting me at that moment how long I had been going for. The silence was unnerving to say the least, swallowing every small thought I had with loud ringing in my ears. Figuring that fidgeting with the radio was pointless after all, I continued on into the abyss of cluttered trees. I had no option of rest or refreshment of any kind. And my eyes had practically evolved into an all natural night vision system.

Around another half hour passed before I started to notice an ever so subtle shift in the terrain. I found myself now fighting on top of everything else, an uphill slope. On both sides of me, the natural brush and wilderness widened out into a field formation, leaving a large strip of bright tall grass illuminated by the full moon. The forest line was now completely visible to me as I entered the grassy field. It was an almost unnatural, and odd cutoff of the trees where the field began, making a wall of forest that stretched for miles along.

I had made my way halfway through the field before the grass started to get shorter and less rugged by each step. I felt the area become more controlled the further I went, going from a wild, unkempt environment, almost to the condition of someone's front lawn. It was then, at that moment, I saw it. The very thing I had risked my life over copious times just to see.

It was the fence.

That's a hardly considerable way to describe it.

For the most part, it took the shape of what I could only imagine the Great Wall of China would look like up close, but in fence form. Due to the way it was colored, it almost perfectly camouflaged itself in with the sky and the rest of its surroundings. My eyes widened at the sight of the colossal structure. Even standing many hundreds of feet away, its presence was intimidating. I closed in on it a bit more to have a better look at what my eyes were having trouble believing.

I couldn't get an exact standpoint due to the distance, but I knew it had to have towered over the forest line. Before I was physically close enough to touch the thing, it's true form fully emerged from the darkness. Hundreds of wide metal pipes, painted as black as the night, protruded from the ground side by side. Each one, suspending smaller beams perpendicular to it, forming a massive grid pattern.

I further noticed as I was no farther than an arm's length away, all of the barbed wire coding it. The texture of the fence was bizarre, in a way that seemed to eat light. I didn't dare try to touch it. Taking a couple steps back to get more of a view of it, I tried my radio again to contact Luna. It took multiple tries of shifting the antenna and fidgeting with the buttons, and I honestly was sure there would be no way it would work. However surprisingly I got a decently clear signal after a minute of trying.

"Luna, you there?" I asked in a hushed tone.

"Yeah" she replied almost instantly.

"I uh, I found the fence, and it's huge. But I'm sure you know."

"How did you get there!? There's only one way there and it takes well over a day to hike to from my place. How could you have..."

"I guess I took a shortcut." I interrupted.

There was a slight pause.

"How come you didn't tell me this was out here? All this time don't you think this is a bit of bigger deal than just a scribble on a map?" I asked frustrated.

"What's the point? Honestly? Do you know how long I've been out here? Seriously do you have any idea?" She sounded almost as upset as I was now.

"I... don't know Luna."

"*Two years*. Going on three. And don't you think that within that time, I've tried many things? Seen things?" She asked rhetorically.

I stayed silent.

She sighed. "Don't you see? That fence is closing us in like animals. And just like animals, there's no way we're getting out. I didn't tell you because I, I wanted you to survive. You would've never made it this far without losing it otherwise."

I couldn't think of any reasonable response. I felt more pressured by stress than ever before in that short moment.

"Ya know... I'm pretty sure whoever else's out there, wants you alive too." She concluded.

"I'm sorry, Luna." I finally responded.

I made my way a bit further down the seemingly infinite wall of metal, towards a flat meadow surrounded by a patch of small bushes. There wasn't any sign of a way through or around it. It penetrated through the tree line a decent ways away from where I was, and continued on into nothingness, forming a slight but noticeable curvature inwards. Everything about the place that

I had spent a considerable amount of my life felt completely wrong from what I thought I knew.

I was trapped.

Encaged.

I had been for months. Yet even all of the memories that slowly came back to me over time could not tell me how I even got here. I sat down in the center of the meadow, beyond any level of exhaustion I had felt before. My body and mind felt utterly defeated. I tossed the radio to my side and collapsed on the soft grassy floor. The only thing in my view bring one mammoth wall, and the arm of the Milky Way with all its glory.

I reflected back on what I'd accomplished, and how I'd come this far. To a dead end. Imagining what Luna might have been doing at that exact moment, and where she could have been brought comfort to me. Perhaps she was thinking the same. I'd humorously expect that after this long together we'd to some extent have linked thoughts. After all, we were just two people surviving. I rubbed my face mindlessly expecting a smooth sensation, only to be met with an unruly beard.

I had changed so much, and learned as well. Everything about my past life were things I never really thought of anymore. My wife, with her voice still echoing within me from time to time, I'd only dismiss as just a voice. The prison, was a mere foggy dream to me. Who'd brought me here, was a question I no longer bothered asking. Luna's muttered voice escaped the radio again.

"Before, all of this started, I mean with me.... I had a well, I guess you can say pretty questionable life." She stated.

I picked up the radio and with some very last bits of strength replied.

"Yeah. Me too."

Moments later she spoke again. Her voice became more somber than I'd ever heard.

"My father was an alcoholic, and my mom too. Not as much though. One day I was walking home from school during my 9th grade year, and my mom came running down the street screaming 'we have to go' 'we have to go.' And she drove me away to some cabin way out in the middle of nowhere. She told me that dad was having another one of his 'episodes' and that we'd have to stay there for a while. We had a whole new life out there, which seemed like an entirely different world to me. I ended up growing up there. My mom taught me how to fish, and scavenge for food if there was ever a situation where I'd have to. She knew I would've eventually. And one day she was right. Turned out my father ended up finding the cabin one late night when I was 19. My mom knew what my father would have done me. She practically threw me out the door and told me to just run. And I did. Years went passed and I never felt like returning to that life I thought was normal. Out here is just, basically who I am. I... I just thought you should know."

The wind started to pick up as she finished her last statement. I felt compelled to express my sorrow for her, but I couldn't formulate how to say it. At that moment it once again dawned on me how much I still didn't know about her, along with how little she must have known about me.

"I'm sorry you had to go through that. Really I am." I finally managed to say.

"Trust me it's not something that I even think about much these days." She replied.

The temperature around me dropped consistently over the course of those few minutes. Whether or not it was my imagination, I felt like it fit the atmosphere. I truly didn't care about making it out. I didn't care about escaping and making it back to my normal life, or even to a life of imprisonment. I only then realized this. All I cared about was simply living. Every struggle, and hardship was nothing more than a stepping stone in the process of living, a new life. In some far off bizarre sense, I wanted it to be my life. No matter how short it would prove to be.

My hands were cold, and barren in the harsh conditions, hardly able to move a finger. I felt the tears freeze into small strips of icicles down to my ears.

I wasn't sad, I hadn't had felt any more at peace with the idea of mortality than at that very instant.

"I guess it's your turn." Said Luna's voice through the radio.

"My... turn... for what?" I struggled to release the words as my voice weakened.

"You know, you never told me exactly where you came from Reg."

I dropped the radio in exhaustion and confusion to what I'd say next. Ideas of how I could explain everything circled through my mind. I had told Luna about my wife, and her death. I never told her anything else. I guess out of pure luck I was able to dodge that question for so long. Nevertheless, I felt it unnecessary to hide it any longer.

"I was a prisoner." I said in one short exhale.

"A prisoner?... For, what?" She asked.

I took a few seconds to reply.

"They falsely convicted me of killing Jessie. No evidence, barely any process. Just, that's it. You're done."

The radio was silent until I broke it once more.

"Death row." I stated.

"And now you're just, here." She responded curiously.

"Yup pretty much." I said with a slight sigh.

The wind was heavy now, mimicking that of the storm months before. It formed a slight whistle through the tall grass meadow behind me.

"I'm sorry I didn't tell you before-"

"Don't worry about it." She interrupted. "Just don't."

The wind started morphing into a strange distant sound that I couldn't identify. It was far, but noticeable.

"You're gonna make it Reggie, you are. Maybe we'll touch bases one day."

"I wish you could be here now, it's an amazing view of the sky." I replied tiresomely.

"Yeah, it's quite a nice view from where I'm at. Small forest fire burning a little ways off, quite the light show."

The thought confused me. Throughout all of the time I'd spent on this adventure, forest fires were something I'd never come across. It never seemed like the season for fires to run amuck in the wilderness. Nevertheless, I pictured the scene. I pictured the vibrant orange and red haze burning over the distant horizon, and a menacing plume of smoke rising from it. An otherworldly scene. Luna's end of the radio was now completely silent. I began imagining the things she could have been doing, and all that she'd done out here in the years she'd spent.

I truly hadn't even seen the beginning of what was out here to experience. I must have come off as some intrusion of her life that just appeared out of nowhere one day. Either that or some random voice that would chatter mindlessly over a radio constantly. I reached out to grab it in an effort to bring it closer to me. The ground around me was colder now than ever before and felt like ice against my worn out body.

In what truly felt like the last moments of life, I began to formulate something I'd say to Luna as a final impression. I knew I couldn't have had much longer in the brittle conditions, along with my already fatigued self. I felt at peace with the idea of dying there, rather than some cold wooden chair. Maybe that was the point of this whole endeavor.

"Maybe we will see each other soon..." Luna's voice came from the radio.

I didn't know what she'd meant by this, or how to have reacted.

"Maybe... what makes you say that?" I managed to reply with the very little amount of breath left.

I rested in silence for what seemed like hours after I asked. I dropped the radio as my arm finally gave way to its condition. Only seconds later she replied.

"I just have a feeling. Good luck Reggie."

The radio cut to dead air once again. Luna must have shut it off on her end afterward. I didn't have the strength to reply. I mustered a simple "Thanks" out loud as I felt myself slowly slipping from consciousness. So much so that I barely noticed the distant buzzing from before become a full on chopping noise.

I lifted my head slightly and adjusted my eyes to a blinding light now blasting in my direction. Along with it came a powerful surge of wind. It surprisingly took me a few seconds to realize a helicopter had just landed mere feet away from me. It's blinding spotlight now lit up the entire meadow and instantly cleared the dried shrubs around me. Regardless of its ground shaking fury, I simply lacked the energy to react fully to it.

Two men emerged from the sliding door and ran towards my position. Clearly they'd been searching for me. Without hesitation, I found myself being literally escorted into the helicopter by my arms and feet and was met with another figure at the entrance who assisted in pulling me in. The interior was well lit, which made it possible to see the people who for some reason showed interest in me up close. The two men that escorted me wore full hazmat suits of some kind. It reminded me of magma suits but without a layer of reflective padding. The third figure was now standing to the side, presumably observing their performance in assisting me to a gurney that was placed next to the wall.

I saw the figure's position change as he gestured for the other men to retrieve something from outside. My consciousness faded in and out over the course of those few minutes. The two suited men eventually returned and started instantly hooking me up to machines. At this point, I knew it was a rescue. The lights above me faded slightly as we gained altitude.

13. ALIVE

I woke up after only a few minutes after takeoff. I hadn't even realized I'd officially gone under until I saw the newly implanted IV tube in my arm. An extremely bright orange light caught my attention from the side window of the sliding door. Outside, I clearly saw that we were passing what seemed to be the fire Luna was talking about. Either it had grown rapidly in a short amount of time, or Luna was vastly underestimating it.

The fire was way larger than I pictured. From inside the helicopter alone, I saw vast extents of the landscape being turned into a bright orange sea. It took full minutes to pass it all. And in the midst of all of it, I almost convinced myself that I saw the cabin, and the ridge slowly burning at the center. Before I was able to study it more, I gasped in surprise as I noticed the man I saw earlier staring at me in the corner of my eye.

"Oh sorry, didn't mean to uh... well, scare you there I guess." He said blissfully.

I just stared back in confusion.

"Not sure if you remember be, but I'm, Randy Keith." The man continued.

"*Officer Keith?*" I had recognized him. Every bit of my memory had returned to me after all.

"Yup..." He gazed out the window as he spoke. "Yeah, that's me. Quite the scene down there huh?" He had a grim expression on his face.

I nodded in reply as he looked over at me.

"Yeah, it was quite the scene for the last couple months over at, well... actually everywhere." He walked next to the large window overlooking the fire.

The helicopter began to make a slight turn, exposing the full extent of the it.

"The whole country's been talking about you, Reggie." He stated. "It's a little bit of an awkward situation of course but... you've been proven innocent." He added and looked back at me.

I was too overloaded with thoughts to respond. He smiled and looked back down at the fire.

"That down there... now that is history in the making." He said as he pointed to it.

I continued my own gaze on the mesmerizing light that was now mostly behind the helicopter. Officer Keith turned towards me completely as we passed the last of it.

"*You* are a soon to be walking piece of history." He said with a blissful expression.

"How did you find me?" I responded with the best voice I could use. It ended up in a mumble of raspy words however.

"Well, it was 6 months Reggie. We have our ways." He answered. "And come on! You really think we're gonna just forget about something as amazing as what you did? The world couldn't forget that even if it tried."

He said now leaning against the wall. His expression faded a bit as noticed my still lackadaisical state. I could hardly find the means to think clearly at that moment, let alone process everything that was happening. He sighed.

"Look, I know you're gonna need some time to figure all this out but... just know, everything's gonna be clear in due time." He stated as he walked off into another compartment of the helicopter.

The room I was in had completely dimmed from its previously bright orange state. Outside, only a dark endless sea of trees that came off as a familiar sight. I had no idea what was going to happen next, or what life would be like after all of it. I decided to spend my last few waking moments clearing my mind of nothing but Luna. Had she been rescued? Was she even alive? I scolded myself for not informing anyone that I was by no means the only one that was in need of a rescue. As much as I knew she loved this life, I couldn't sit right with the idea of simply leaving her out there. Regardless of whether she was or not. The rest of the ride through the darkening night was a series of bumps and turbulence. It seemed like hours before I finally found myself under the soothing control of sleep.

I woke up to the sliding door of the helicopter opening abruptly. The morning rays of sunshine overwhelmed the cabin. I partially sat up before realizing that we had already landed. The two men from before entered into the cabin again from outside and without speaking a word, proceeded to undo all of the electronics and IV bags around me. I had the nerve to ask them a simple question out of my curiosity.

"Where are we?" Were the first coherent words I'd spoken in a decent while.

One of the men who was closest to me simply looked up and slightly grinned.

"Houston." He said and continued his duties.

I tried moving and hoisting myself up anxiously.

"Woah there buddy... take it easy." Officer Keith ordered as he emerged from the cockpit.

"You've been through quite a bit already. Just slow down a bit and be easy on yourself." He said and walked out.

Outside in the distance I noticed another helicopter parked parallel to mine. From what I could tell, it was almost identical as well. A few minutes passed before the two workers had completely unhooked me from God knows how many machines. One of them stopped before walking out and looked back.

"You need any help sir?" He asked earnestly.

"I'm quite alright. Thanks." I replied.

At that he hopped out of the helicopter and met up with officer Keith and another figure I couldn't make out.

I eventually managed to stand up and make my way to the sliding door.

The early morning sun was blinding. Officer Keith finished his conversation and looked up at me. Without delay he gestured over to something behind him and smiled back at me. I thought I was hallucinating at the sight of it. The second figure was holding on to a dog. But it wasn't just a dog, it was Malos.

I instantly recognized him. Something was different about him however. The animal's ora had completely changed from what I remembered. Going from a true wild scavenger, to an almost completely domesticated dog. It started wagging its tail sporadically at the sight of me.

"One of our teams picked him up near the source of the fire while we were looking for you." Keith said looking down at Malos.

"Source... of the fire?" I questioned.

"Yeah, possible arson, most likely the case to be honest." He answered with a more somber tone.

"You know where it started?" I asked.

He paused for a moment before answering. He frowned and glanced back at the officer behind him, then looked back at me.

"Just a small cabin. Went up like a stack of hay. Strange bump in the night." He replied hesitantly.

I could tell even he was weirded out by just the thought of it.

"He's all yours by the way. If you want of course." Keith said as he nodded towards the dog. "He barely made it out of there alive you know." He continued.

The officer released him and at an instant, rushed towards me. Keith smirked at the sight.

"He seems to have a liking to you for some reason." He said scratching his head.

The other mustached officer then patted Keith on the shoulder and tapped on his watch. I felt like asking more to satisfy my still unruly sense of confusion, but I resisted myself.

"Common, let's get you all cleaned up and ready to go." Keith told me as he motioned to follow him.

"Oh yeah, and one more thing." He stopped and reached for something in his back pocket. He pulled out the radio and handed it to me. "Thought you should keep that too." He said as I examined it thoroughly.

It was definitely my radio.

I nodded and smiled. He patted my back and walked me off the heliport.

I was led into a small but extremely cozy looking building off the side of some other small choppers. The inside stored a completely different vibe. Keith motioned once again at me towards some of the waiting room chairs. I took my seat as I saw him disappear down the hallway. The room I was in was bright, and enlightening. A full glass wall behind me created a view to the entire port. My eyes wandered towards a clock hanging from the top corner of the room. I realized that it was my first opportunity in months to actually know the time.

8:32 it read.

It truly felt nice to see those numbers. I didn't have much time to myself before another figure stepped out of the hallway and into my view. To my disbelief, it was the red suited man from ages ago, wearing predictably, the red suit that looked cleaner than in my memory. He smiled and walked towards my area when he noticed me.

"Hi Reggie." He said as he sat across from me.

Everything about the vibe he gave off was extremely familiar to me. He sat nonchalauntly leaning forward with that awkward expression I remembered from the last time I'd seen him.

"So I assume you've come to understand the basics of the situation by now right?" He asked happily and folded his hands. He waited patiently with a forced grin for a response.

"I broke outta prison, and lived in the forest for half of a year. What more is there to know?" I answered.

"And uh, maybe we should be the ones offering our formal apology." He said as he sat back. "I know that means pretty much... well nothing, but hey, I think this whole thing was a learning experience for both ends." He continued.

I simply nodded in response.

His remorse felt sincere as he gazed off in the distance.

"Oh, and as late as it may be, I just want to say, I'm sorry for your loss Reggie." He looked back at me with compassion. Something I'd never witnessed in the few short times I'd encountered the man. After all, I still didn't know his name, nor really anything about him. I didn't feel the need to ask however. A few seconds went by before either one of us broke the silence. When he did, his expression instantly changed from charismatic to happy go lucky once again.

"So, how was your experience at the 20th parallel?" He asked.

The question shocked me. I'd didn't know how he could have possibly known what the 20th parallel even was. Regardless, I answered him trying to hide my concerns the best I could.

"It was... great." I said with a half forced smile.

"Fantastic." He replied.

He instantly sat up again.

"You should probably go shave that gnarly beard now eh?" He said standing up.

I got up in agreement and felt it. It had honestly felt even longer than when I'd last checked. The red suited man chuckled.

"We got all you need in the bathroom down the hall." He exclaimed.

At that, I started to make my way down.

I walked out of room feeling like an entirely different person. My face alone had felt like it lost weight. I felt my now smooth and hairless face as I met up with the red suited man at the main room. His eyes widened as he saw me.

"Damn. Now that's the Reggie I remember." He said with a surprised expression.

Officer Keith was sitting near him with a similar face, the last time he'd seen my face like this, was the last time he thought he'd see me alive. The red suited man got up and patted me on the back.

"It's gonna be awhile before you fully recover from this. Just take it easy for now." He said in a hushed tone.

"It's probably gonna be a while until I get used to this life again too." I said in a broken voice.

"*You will.*" He said with a wide grin.

He turned towards officer Keith.

"Uh, Randy, please could you take Mr. Green here down to the parking lot? Oh also, fetch em some water would you?"

Keith compiled and escorted me.

"Just take it one step at a time Reg!" The red suited man shouted from down the hallway as we made to the elevator.

He vanished as quick as he appeared after that. His final impression on me left me with lasting questions about him, and still left me anerved. Keith eyed me while in the elevator and mumbled one sentence to me.

"I'm glad you did it."

I looked over at him as the elevator slowed down. Before I could respond, the doors opened and revealed Malos lying patiently near the parking lot. He instantly sprung up and ran to us in excitement.

"That's your gift to remember all this by I guess." Keith said as Malos energetically jumped on me.

He truly was a loyal companion to me. Moments passed of this before I noticed the one and only vehicle sitting in the lot. In the far right corner, I saw my very own truck, exactly the same as what I had left behind. By the looks of it, the truck very well seemed to be in better condition as well. Keith must have seen me catch sight of it.

"Yeah, that's your other gift." He exclaimed as he walked out.

He walked to the back of the truck and reached for something in the bed. I followed along with a still excited Malos trailing behind me. Keith turned back at me and handed me keys that looked like they belonged to car fresh out of the dealership.

"She's all yours." He said with the same cheeky grin he always seemed to have.

I took them gratefully.

Keith whistled to Malos and pulled down the tailgate of the truck. Without hesitation, the dog jumped in, and settled down near the front.

"So what's your next adventure gonna be boss?" Keith questioned.

"I guess whatever it is, it'll choose me again." I answered.

I hopped into the truck and examined it, hoping to find some instance of my previous self. The whole thing had been wiped clean, and spotless. No nick or cranny was cluttered or dirty. I placed the radio in the center console and sat back, reminiscing in the memories of the truck. Before I pulled out, Keith walked up to the window again and simply prompted a hand shake.

"Happy trails partner!" Was the last thing he said to me before I peeled out of the lot.

I looked back at the station as I came to the Main Street intersection. I only got a mere glimpse of it before Malos stood up and blocked my view. The dog looked at me through the window with the same joyful expression. I smiled back and turned on the am radio tuner that had never even worked before in the truck.

Instantly "Goin' Down The Road Feelin Bad" by Cliff Carlisle met my ears. The upbeat tone of the music calmed my nerves.

As I merged onto the main interstate, I glanced down at the radio again. I knew it was something that I would keep as a memento of

Luna. Wherever she may have been, Something deep within me knew she was safe, and contempt with herself. It was only then when I fully realized that she never really needed me. I served as nothing more than a friend to her, and a distant voice. Nevertheless, the radio would always sit in my truck.

I would never touch it, or move it, or even think about it much. It was just simply there. It was a part of me.

I decided to relax myself, and clear my mind. I figured I might as well begin to enjoy life again, so I decided to take the long country route home. After all, I always had a liking to the great outdoors.

79352808R00099

Made in the USA
Middletown, DE
09 July 2018